For Avery,
Wilbur, the
magic Wise One,
told me that
you are going
to have wonderful
magical adventures.
Nancy Yolse

THE CRYSTAL NAVIGATOR

A PERILOUS JOURNEY BACK
THROUGH TIME

NANCY KUNHARDT LODGE

Cover Illustration: Evi Gstottner

Published by Wilwahren Press

First Edition

ISBN 13   978-0-9960885-2-7

Library of Congress Control Number: 2014937529

This book is dedicated to my Corgi, Wilbur, a gentle Wise One, who sat me down one day and told me a story.

"The world is full of magic things, patiently waiting for our senses to grow sharper."
— W.B. Yeats

TABLE OF CONTENTS

Chapter 1

Omens

Lucy Nightingale was just coming to the best part of her oral report about General Hannibal crossing the Alps when a loud honking noise startled her so badly that her notes flew out of her hands. Victor Snorkle, the grossest boy in class, was blowing his nose. Her notes lay scattered on the gritty floor, too smudged to read. From then on, things went from awful to unbelievably horrible.

The sixth grade teacher, Velma Dawson, was the meanest teacher in the school. She was just like a witch with her lumpy stockings and witchy shoes, and her long, grey braid that she wound around her whole head. The second Lucy stopped talking Miss Dawson's head jerked up and she pointed her laser beam eyes at Lucy.

"Class?" Miss Dawson said in a shrill voice. "Tell Lucy that we are waiting."

"We're waiting, Loocy," repeated the class in unison.

Her classmates stared at her, a couple of them whispered, Victor sneered. *I can't stand it*, thought Lucy. *They're laughing at me.*

Her face stung with embarrassment and her stomach hurt. Then she was on the floor and someone who smelled like Juicy Fruit life savers was breathing on her face. Lucy opened her eyes and looked into the powdery, pink face of Miss Herbert, the nice school nurse, and beyond Miss Herbert, a circle of the stunned faces of her classmates.

Victor shoved his way into the circle, took one look at her, and said, "She's a goner."

A goner, thought Lucy. *He's right. Part of me is gone.*

The confident part of herself, the Lucy who loved school, the Lucy who could give perfect oral reports and got A's, that Lucy had walked out on her. She would probably not get another A this year. She lay on the dirty floor and wished for something, anything at all, to happen that would make her problems disappear.

The next morning, Lucy wore her favorite blue dress with the zippered pockets and lace up silver boots. She worried about having to face Miss Dawson. What if she fainted just by looking at her? Lucy was standing in front of her mirror braiding her waist-length red hair when something peculiar happened. Reflected in the mirror, a soft yellow light glowed from inside the bookcase behind her. At first she did not see it because the light was growing dimmer. Hidden behind one of the quartz crystals

2

that lined the bookshelves, her fingers found a small, rectangular crystal still pulsing with light.

Lucy knew more about quartz crystals than most grownups and she had never seen one as beautiful as this one. It was flat with glassy surfaces and beveled edges, and it was absolutely clear except for the gold needles shooting through it. The needles glittered in the morning sun. When she closed her fingers around it, she felt warm and happy. There was something special about a crystal that had just appeared as if by magic. She dropped it into one of her zippered pockets so the next time something bad happened she could hold it and feel normal again.

Before she left her room, Lucy hung a blue flash drive around her neck and grabbed a sweater. She took one last look around to make sure everything was as it should be, but things were not as they should be. Something weird was going on with the big crystals on her bookshelf. They sat in a straight row on the shelf, but their jagged shadows were pointing in the wrong direction. This was a scientific impossibility and scientific impossibilities must happen for a reason. Could these backwards shadows be omens about something bad in her future? Maybe witchy Miss Dawson was sending her some sort of horrible message. The only person who would know what the wrong way shadows meant was her best friend, Sam Winter.

Sam and Lucy had been friends since he moved next door when they were both five years old. Unlike Lucy, Sam did not care about grades or what people thought about him, and he was not the least bit interested in pleasing his teachers. His rocket scientist parents agreed with him about practically everything, especially about school, which Sam thought was a huge inconvenience. He spent all his free time collecting vintage communication gadgets that he used to invent new ones. His latest theories had to do with molecules and brain waves. Maybe it was because he was an expert communicator, but Sam could hear all kinds of unusual things that non-geniuses could not hear. Lucy had even heard him carry on long conversations with his dopey, psychic sheepdog, Doppler.

When Lucy got to the bus stop that morning, Sam's angular body seemed to have fallen headfirst against a tree. As she got closer, she saw that he was squinting through a magnifying glass at some sort of yellow mold.

Without turning his head, he said, "I know you're there, Lucy."

"Yuk," she said, looking over his shoulder, "Why would you be interested in disgusting sap oozing out of a tree?"

Sam gave her a blank look then said, "Because, this is a new kind of sap that's not listed in 'Den Vinter Svampe', which is the Danish authority on the saps of the world. Since I discovered it, it'll be named after me. Isn't that the most awesome thing you've ever heard?"

4

Lucy rolled her eyes whenever Sam spoke Danish. "Do you honestly think that goo hasn't already been discovered? Wait, don't answer that; I hear the bus coming, but, if you want to save that glop, you better put it into a test tube or whatever."

Lucy hoisted her backpack onto her shoulders just as the wheezing school bus squealed to a stop in front of them. Sam quickly scraped off some of the rare sap and smeared it in a glass tube.

When they were settled on the bus, Lucy said, "Do things feel different today? Like something creepy might have happened?"

Sam's head jerked up from the test tube he was labeling.

"Creepy? In what way, creepy?"

The bus bumped over a pothole, jostling them on the hard seats. Lucy grabbed the bar on the back of the seat in front of her.

Lowering her voice, she said, "Creepy, like if I happened to see some backwards shadows."

Sam smiled widely and stuck his face so close to hers that her eyes crossed.

"You actually saw a chromatic aberration?"

"Yes, I think that's exactly what I saw," she said. "My crystals were casting backwards shadows this morning. Do you think it means something bad? Like that old Miss Dawson is going to stab me with her ruler or give me F's all year?"

Sam stared at the ceiling of the bus and thought for a moment.

"Well? What do you think?" Lucy asked.

He said, "I don't think disobedient shadows predict stabbings. Mostly, they're known for foretelling a perilous journey."

Lucy shivered. Perilous journeys meant storms at sea or falling out of a hot air balloon. She leaned her head against the open window beside her seat and closed her eyes. The wind rushed across her face, blowing her hair back in flat sheets. *Wait a minute*, she thought. *Maybe the disobedient shadows pointed to something exciting in my future, like a treasure hunt.* That was the safest, least scary way to think about it.

The bus skidded sideways on a carpet of wet leaves before coming to a stop in front of Beverly Middle School. Lucy really dreaded seeing Miss Dawson again, but when she crossed the threshold of the classroom, the teacher's chair was empty. Miss Dawson did not seem to be lurking in the corners of the room either.

"Where is she?" Lucy said.

Sam shrugged and said, "Who cares?" He was not remotely interested in the whereabouts of any teacher. He took off his glasses and rubbed his eyes. Without them, Sam's eyebrows pinched together giving him a worried look. His pale hair hung over his forehead in blunt ribbons that slid under his glasses and poked into his eyes.

"You're so lucky you don't have to wear glasses," he said.

"Actually, I've been thinking about getting some clear ones to make me look smarter," Lucy replied.

Sam sighed. "That's just silly. You are plenty smart enough. Who cares if you look smart?"

"I do," Lucy said. "They might make my brain work faster."

"Oh please. If your brain worked any faster, it might short circuit. You have inordinately fast synapses firing simultaneously."

"Okay, what are synapses?"

"They're miniscule circuit breakers in the brain that unclutter your mind so you can focus huge amounts of energy on one thing," said Sam.

Even though she did not understand why synapses and circuit breakers were important, it made her feel better because Sam believed it.

Sam carried all his school things in a battered, old briefcase that had belonged to his grandfather. He hauled out a heavy book, entitled *The Steady Gaze of Tawosret's Mummy* and held it up in front of his eyes, whispering as he read.

Lucy thought the title did not make sense.

"You know there aren't any holes in mummy rags so old what's-his-name's mummy couldn't have gazed steadily or wobbly," she said.

Sam inserted a finger between the pages of the book and said, "The gaze doesn't refer to the actual mummy. In fact, there's no such thing as mummy holes. The author probably invented them because they sound ghoulish."

"So where's the gaze coming from?" she said.

Sam pointed to the statue on the cover of the book and said, "The Egyptian pharaohs were buried in tombs inside the pyramids. They didn't like the idea of lying in boring mummy rags for centuries so they put huge statues with scary crystal eyes in their tombs."

"Cool, but why would that...?"

Sam interrupted her. "The minute everyone left the pyramid, the king's spirit floated out of the mummy rags and jumped inside one of the statues. From inside the statue, he could see the happy scenes from his life painted on the walls."

"Oh I get it," said Lucy. "It's the steady gaze of the *spirit* of the pharaoh looking through the statue's crystal eyeballs."

"Precisely."

Lucy rested her chin in her hands and said, "My mom told me that after the pharaoh had been dead in his tomb a few hundred years, his spirit rode up to the stars in a magic boat."

Sam nodded and said, "He must have used the tunnels to fly to the stars."

Lucy's head popped up. "What tunnels?"

"They were more like air shafts leading from the tomb to the outside of the pyramid. It's how the tomb robbers got in and robbed all the gold thrones and cats."

Lucy checked her glow-in-the-dark IWatch.

"Miss Dawson shouldn't be late. I'm positive there's a law in the Teacher's Handbook that says a teacher should not be out gallivanting around so close to class time."

"She is not gallivanting around," said Sam. "If you must know, Miss Dawson is nowhere near the school today. There's

9

another teacher right outside the room having a conversation with someone who is invisible."

Lucy gaped at him. "What?"

She knew Sam talked to Doppler in dog language and she knew he could hear unusual things, but she had never heard him listen to a conversation between a real person and an invisible someone.

"Miss Dawson would never talk to someone who wasn't standing within stabbing distance. She'd thwack anyone who dared to be invisible with her ruler," said Lucy.

"It's *not* her," Sam said. "It's someone new, someone peculiar."

"How do you know someone is invisible if you can't even see him?"

"I can tell because whoever is out there sounds sort of hollow."

Lucy wondered what hollow sounded like.

"So what are they talking about?" She asked.

"I don't know," said Sam. "They're speaking a language that doesn't have any pronouns or transitive verbs."

"How do you know these things, Sam?"

"I don't know how I know them. I just do, alright? Turn around, she's coming."

11

Chapter 2

Miss Arabella Lang

The handle turned, the door opened, and a woman who looked the opposite of a teacher floated into the classroom. Her blond hair was swept up in a perfect French twist. Her silver shoes sparkled, and her dress swished as she crossed the classroom to the teacher's desk. A red Santa Claus-type sack hung from her shoulder.

Lucy blinked. This was not a regular person. She had magic written all over her. The woman sat on the teacher's desk and crossed her legs. The silver shoe that dangled from one of her toes hypnotized Lucy. The beautiful woman turned a brilliant smile on the eager faces of the students and said, "My name is Arabella Lang. I am tickled pink to be your teacher while Miss Dawson is away."

Away? Lucy wondered. *Forever?*

"What fun we'll have," Miss Lang said, happily. "Wait until you see my homework assignments. You're going to love them."

Lucy had never heard a teacher talk about school and fun at the same time and she had definitely never loved homework. There was so much pressure to do it perfectly.

Sam stopped tapping his glass fountain pen against his teeth long enough to say, "Absolutely fascinating."

Miss Lang said, "You must be thinking 'this teacher is a nutcase.' Who ever heard of fun homework?"

This sounded like a trick question. The students nodded then thought better of it and shook their heads.

"Certainly, you will like learning from me," Miss Lang said. "But the real fun is learning from each other. What could be more fascinating than seeing the world through another person's eyes?"

The students nodded then shrugged their shoulders. This teacher was hard to follow.

Miss Lang hopped off the desk and said, "Now it's time for the party."

"What party?" Lucy said.

Sam shrugged.

Miss Lang said, "I whipped up my famous pineapple upside down cake just for you. Pineapples are wonderful icebreakers, don't you think?"

She reached into her sack and lifted out a cake covered with pineapples, a pitcher of lemonade, and a bunch of horns. Then she cut the cake into even pieces and put everything on a tray which she began to pass around.

Lucy's classmates looked like nodding robots. Sam poked her with his glasses.

"Ow, what's the matter?" She said.

"What kind of a teacher wastes time handing out cake and horns?"

"The cool kind, be quiet," she whispered.

While the students ate their cake, Miss Lang rummaged around in her sack muttering to herself.

"Fiddlesticks. Where did I put those whatchamacallits?"

She scrabbled in her sack through what must be all sorts of cool things until finally she said, "Oh good, here they are," and held up a bunch of pale blue envelopes with the students' names written on the front in swirly script.

When everyone had gobbled up every last crumb of the cake, Miss Lang held up the envelopes and said, "Your first assignment is to prepare a short PowerPoint presentation about the subject enclosed in your envelope."

This was the one thing Lucy never wanted to hear again. After her humiliating experience yesterday, she dreaded giving another oral report.

"Do not exchange questions or invent a question you like better," Miss Lang said. "I designed each question just for you and, if you follow my directions, you won't get lost."

A light in one of Miss Lang's blue eyes twinkled. She glided from desk to desk, slapping the envelopes down with the flat of her palm.

When Lucy read her question, Miss Lang's pretty blue paper started rattling in her hands. This wonderful teacher had given her an impossible assignment. Lucy's question was:

"What do these five paintings tell you about the personality of the artist: Botticelli's _Primavera_, Leonardo da Vinci's _Mona Lisa_, Michelangelo's _Sistine Ceiling_,

Jacopo Pontormo's *Four Women,* and Vincent van Gogh's *Starry Night?*"

"I know your ideas will be wonderful because they will be original," said Miss Lang.

Lucy held her head in her hands and moaned. *My ideas? I don't think I have any wonderful ideas. Not only that, my mind will probably go blank again.* This assignment was worse than long division.

Sam tapped her on the shoulder. "What's the matter?"

"I'll tell you later, but it's bad. It has to do with being empty-handed."

15

Chapter 3

The Wise Ones

Later that afternoon, Lucy and Sam stood looking up at the massive oak tree that supported his elaborate tree house. A rickety staircase connected the main room to an open-air turret. The tree house was Sam's work place where he stored the remnants of old inventions that he used to make new ones. Sam unhooked a rope ladder and they climbed up to the cluttered workroom. The junk he collected must have doubled since the last time Lucy had been in the tree house. She picked up a rusty tin thing between her thumb and index finger.

"Why are you keeping this revolting, old thing?"

"That might look like a rotted flour sifter to you, but it's actually the prototype of an automatic hardboiled egg peeler," he said.

"Okay, but why do you want to *keep* it?"

Sam stared at her for a minute then he took off his glasses and pointed them at her.

"What you have to realize, Lucy, is that every new invention is teeming with the vibrating, genius-laden molecules of its inventor."

Lucy spread her arms out, palms up. "Okay, so what?"

"I've told you before, if you touch an invention long enough, the inventor's molecules will wriggle through your skin and swim right into your brain," Sam said.

"Can't you please just answer my question?" Lucy persisted. "Why do you care about the molecules of the nincompoop, who invented a stupid hardboiled egg peeler?"

"That nincompoop was light years ahead of his time," said Sam, walking to the other side of the room. "Come over here. I want to show you my newest experiment."

Lucy sighed, set down the egg peeler, and joined him across the room. They sat on high stools in front of a long plywood board attached to one side of the tree house. On it was a tray of crystals and a complicated-looking contraption.

Lucy held one of the crystals up to her eye. Twisting it toward the light, she asked, "Did you dig these out of the earth?"

"No, I bought them on the Internet. They come from a mountain in Montana."

"Well they gypped you," she said, tossing the crystal back on the tray. "They're all cloudy."

"So what, they're perfectly good?"

"Sam," said Lucy, "if you're going to buy a crystal, you should always talk to me first. You should never buy one because of some fake picture on the Internet."

"Forget what they look like," he said. "That doesn't make any difference as far as I'm concerned. The only important thing is that they are the right size and shape for conducting radio waves. Look."

He pointed to his experiment. It consisted of copper wire, a lever, a small cloudy crystal, a tiny light bulb, a battery, and a tuning fork.

Lucy's long hair had worked its way out of the braid and was now entangled in the wire.

"This thing with the fork looks pretty cool," she said, fiddling with the lever.

"Collect all that hair, will you?" He said, lifting her hand off the lever and depositing it as far from the mechanism as possible.

She extricated her hair from the components of Sam's whateveritwas and wound it into a knot on top of her head.

"Okay, now pay attention," he said. "This thing is not just cool. It's very cool. It's a radio and that is the crystal that transmits the radio waves."

"That's awesome! But, are you positive that crystals can do that?" Lucy asked.

"Absolutely, and, if you ask me, that's the only reason you need them."

"I don't think that's right," she said, frowning. "I have an amazing crystal with gold slivers running through it that makes me feel happy, so it must have a life force."

Sam gave her a blank look and said, "The only thing that gives crystals life force is electric currents."

"Why would you electrify it?" She asked.

"Because when you shoot an electric current through a crystal, it wobbles up and down like a wave, like this."

Sam made a wave-like motion with his hand.

"Mm-hmm," Lucy said, resting her chin on her fists. This discussion was starting to put her to sleep.

Sam kept talking. "A wobbling, electrocuted crystal puts out wavelengths that look for other wavelengths that wobble at the same speed. When it finds one, the two wavelengths can communicate with each other."

Lucy sat bolt upright. Sam had finally said something interesting.

"Wavelengths?" she said. "Wait, that reminds me of something important. Shoot, I can't remember."

She slid off the stool and said, "Can I show you my report question?"

"Sure, let's go up to the turret," said Sam, leading her up the stairway.

The afternoon was warm and summery and perfect for one of those exciting conversations about big problems. Lucy and Sam sat on a wraparound bench built around the inside wall of the turret. High above the ground, amidst the leafy branches, their voices drifted into the warm afternoon air.

"What's the problem?" Sam asked.

"Okay, you know how important it is for me to get an A, right?"

"Right."

"Well, this time it's going to be impossible because no human could answer Miss Lang's question. Here," she said, shoving the blue paper into Sam's ink-stained fingers. Another one of his quirks was insisting on using an old fashioned fountain pen.

He stared so hard at the paper that he actually dozed off.

"Sam!" Lucy pounded her fist on the bench.

His eyes popped open.

"What?" He shouted.

"What do you think of my question?"

"Oh, right, your question. Sorry. It's easy. All you have to do is look at each painting until it makes you feel happy, or sad, or angry, or whatever. Then you'll know what each artist was like."

"No, that's no good," Lucy said. "That would only be guessing and I'm not going to guess what a bunch of geniuses were like. I have to *know*."

"What would it take to know?" He asked.

She thought for a moment. "I guess I would have to talk to the artists in person, make friends with them. But that's impossible because they lived a long time ago."

"Then you have a dilemma," he said.

"What I need is a guide who can take me back in time."

Lucy smacked her forehead. "Oh my gosh now I remember why wavelengths are important. Radios aren't the only things that use them. Remember the Wise Ones we believed in when we were little; those magic beings who listen for children's wishes with their wavelengths?"

"Of course I do and I still believe every child has his own Wise One that he can contact if he wishes with all his might," Sam said.

"They can't hear unless thoughts are vivid enough to land on their wavelength. Do you think I can do that?" Lucy asked.

"Lucy," said Sam, "you're what I call a high frequency thinker. In fact, I think you could probably make something just by thinking about it."

She looked up through the spreading branches of the oak tree. Splintered beams of sunlight filtered through the leaves, dazzling her eyes. She slapped her thighs and said, "I'll do it. I'll contact a Wise One tonight."

As she climbed down the rope ladder, Sam called, "Let me know if something happens."

She waved and jumped the last four feet to the ground.

Chapter 4

Wilbur

Later that night Lucy sat at her window thinking about the best way to contact a Wise One. A luminous full moon flooded her room with silvery light. Zillions of twinkling stars crowded the velvet sky. The air was warm and filled with the smells of newly mown grass and chrysanthemums. She reached out the window and swept her palm in a wide arc across the sky. It might have been the fierce beauty of the night or it could have been magic pulling at her but, at that moment, Lucy knew that the best place to send her wish was outside under the stars. She climbed out her window, wriggled down the wisteria vine that grew up the side of her house, and jumped to the ground, her bare feet sinking into the night-soaked grass.

Lucy stood on the open lawn under the vast sky. Moonlight bathed the grass, trees, and flowers in blue light, only the woods on the edge of the lawn receded into darkness. Sam had told her that she had enough energy in her mind to make things. All she had to do was think very hard. She focused all that energy on her wish- a tall, kindly Wise One wearing a pointy hat and long white robe with a glowing walking stick leading her through the doors of time and she imagined an artist's sunny studio, smelling of lemony oil paints and metallic turpentine, unfinished paintings propped on easels, tables covered with jars of brushes and palettes smeared with brightly colored paints. In her

22

mind's eye, she saw an artist's hand sweeping a brush across a canvas, creating landscapes with mountains and streams. She concentrated with all the vibrating molecules in her mind on making these pictures real. With the night breezes on her face, Lucy could even imagine what it would feel like to fly.

Something light and feathery quivering in her clenched hand jolted her concentration. She slowly uncurled her fingers and could not believe her eyes. She must have wished especially hard because a blue and gold butterfly sat on her palm looking right at her and twitching its antennae. Now, Lucy knew that Sam had been right. She could make things with her thoughts. She had not wished for it, but a butterfly might be the best way to carry her wish to a Wise One. She lifted her hand and watched its blue and gold wings disappear into the night.

Lucy ran back to her house, climbed into her room, and sat at the window hoping for some sign that a Wise One had heard her. Then, it happened. A cloud, as transparent as a fairy's wing, drifted in front of the moon. As it fluttered by, she heard a voice whisper, "I heard you and you will find me." Relieved and happy, she climbed into bed and swam into dreamland.

Lucy woke up with a start. She had on the same silver boots, blue dress, white sweater, and even the flash drive that she had worn to school yesterday. But was it yesterday? She was not sure. Something was not quite right. The sun blazed in the sky, but it still felt like nighttime. *Strange*, she thought. Outside, it was a beautiful morning. Tiny droplets of dew sparkled as they

23

evaporated in the sun. The green leaves of the maple trees shimmered like emeralds and the purple leaves of the copper beech trees fluttered like pennies in the wind. The rustling of the leaves sounded like a voice whispering, 'The woods are waiting for you.' This was the second time she had heard a voice whispering to her. The voice last night had said 'You will find me.' He must have meant she would find him in the woods. Lucy knew that this moment was the beginning of a miraculous adventure back in time.

Lucy burst through the front door into blinding sunlight. The colors of a thousand dancing flowers dazzled her eyes. In a flash, she was off. Past the rose garden, past the tangled vines of the tomato plants and the honeysuckle hedge, she ran as fast as she could. The wind cooled her face and blew her hair into wavy ropes. Her flash drive thumped from side to side on her chest. She flew onto a red path, one she had never seen before, into the woods. Something brushed across her eyelids. *Cobwebs*, she thought, but they were not like any cobwebs she had known.

Lucy walked alongside marshland thick with swaying pussy willows. She wound her way deep into the woods. Beams of light filtered through the tops of tall evergreens and danced on the ground. Gradually, the red path turned white and powdery, billowing like glittery smoke with her every step. The warm, yellow sunlight deepened into an eerie orange light that cast spiky shadows on the ground. Lucy's only company was the occasional hoot of an owl and the sounds of nocturnal animals scratching for

24

food. She imagined the yellow eyes of hungry creatures watching her, probably thinking of the best way to cook her. Part of her wanted to turn around and run home. Lucy longed for the comfort of her mother's arms around her. But the other part knew there was no turning back from this adventure that had been her wish. She needed to meet the artists to get an A, and she needed an A to get back her confidence. Even so, she was afraid of the orange light and the scratching noises. Just as she felt she might burst into tears the sound of someone sweetly humming drifted from deep in the forest.

"Is someone there?" She called, hoping for a fairy or even a friendly farmer. "I'm scared. If you're nearby, Wise One, please come out and talk to me."

A gentle voice answered her. "Child, your wish will be granted."

Lucy spun around three times searching for the owner of the voice. On the third turn Lucy was shocked to find a black and white Corgi leaning casually against the tree in front of her. He had big paws, short legs, a bushy tail, and a mouth that curled upwards in a funny smile that never went away. Most curious, he was reading a brochure called *Order Your Liquid Mirrors Now!* Her legs felt like spaghetti and her feet felt rooted to the ground. She had not expected a dog, much less a dog who could read brochures about liquid mirrors, whatever they were. This cute little dog could not possibly be a Wise One, could he? Wise Ones are towering and majestic. They wear long robes and wizard hats

25

and carry knobby walking sticks. Maybe the dog was going to take her to the real Wise One.

The Corgi smiled at her over gold-rimmed spectacles. He stuffed the brochure into a fur pocket at his waist and slipped his glasses into another fur pocket on his chest. Then he pitched forward and trotted over to her. She had to admit that he was adorable with his smiley face and short, crooked legs that angled outward like duck's feet.

He stopped in front of her, extended a silky paw, and said, "Welcome, Lucy Nightingale. I am Wilbur, your own personal Wise One."

What? Lucy backed up, just a little. Her mind raced with questions. Was it physically possible for dogs to talk? Did they even have voice boxes? *Well,* she thought, *in situations as unusual as this one, it was probably best to act normal.* She cleared her throat, bent way over, and shook his silky paw.

"It's nice to meet you, your majesty. You can talk, which is wonderful. I'm all for talking dogs. And, it's such a good idea to have actual pockets in your fur."

"No need for majesty," Wilbur said. "Yes, I speak many languages and everyone has pockets somewhere." He studied her and said, "My dear, are you quite well? You look somewhat sick."

"I'm fine," Lucy croaked. "It's just that I expected you to look like a wizard with a flowing beard and a white hat."

Wilbur furrowed his brow, which was as close as he could get to a frown because his mouth curved upward all the time.

"Wizard? Wizard?" He said. "Wizards do not impress me one little bit. Their methods are too old fashioned and don't even talk to me about finding one. You have to jump through funnels to get near their zip code."

"Well, how did you get here?" Lucy asked.

"Never mind how I got here," he said. "I came because you asked me to and it sounded like an emergency. That butterfly you sent slammed into the softest part of my tummy. It still hurts."

This made no sense to Lucy so she changed the subject. "Was that you humming?"

"I'm famous for my humming," he said, proudly.

There he goes again. Can't he just say 'yes?' She thought.

Lucy put her hands on her hips and said, "Can't you just say 'yes' or 'no?'

Wilbur's mouth curled into a smile.. Then Lucy noticed his eyes. She bent over to get a better look.

"Hey, that's cool," she said. "One of your eyes is blue. Let me look at it for a minute."

Wilbur stood still while she inspected his eyes. One was velvety brown; the other was as blue as a summer sky.

She squinted into his blue eye and said, "I think I can see my face, but it's very blurry."

Wilbur said, "The longer we are together, the clearer your reflection will become."

Lucy had no idea what he meant. Was he incapable of giving her a direct answer?

She said, "Is that code for something because it doesn't make sense?"

"Wait a minute," said Lucy, "You haven't told me if you're going to fulfill my wish. I distinctly said I have to go back to meet the artists for my assignment. Are you going to do that? Just say 'yes' or 'no.'"

She was determined to wangle a proper answer from him.

"That will enter into the trip," said Wilbur, trotting into the woods.

"I'm sorry," said Lucy, stumbling after him, "But could you please give me a specific answer to my exact question."

Wilbur produced a miniature manicure kit from a fur pocket.

Buffing a toenail, he said "No, I do not think I will give you such an answer. You're a little too fond of 'specifically this' and 'exactly that.'"

Lucy explained that she only wanted people and talking dogs to give specific answers to her questions. Wilbur listened to her patiently as she talked, staring at her with wide, innocent eyes.

"My answers are all you need", he said while slipping his toenail clippers into a fur pocket. "Now, let's be on our way."

But, he still hasn't answered my most important question, thought Lucy. She was becoming frustrated and a little angry. She watched Wilbur hop like a rabbit through the dark woods. Following the blazing white fur of his paws and the tip of his flickering tail, Lucy jogged along beside him.

"Could you slow down a little and listen to me?"

Wilbur slowed down and now he looked like a rocking horse. Lucy thought maybe she ought to try to ask her questions in a different way. Maybe then he would understand her.

"What do you mean when you say enter into it? Please, Wilbur," she said. "Let's get to wherever it is we're going so you can rev up your best time machine."

Wilbur screeched to a halt. His smiley mouth looked crooked. His eyes were slits. Motioning for her to bend down, he stuck his nose so close to her face that her eyes crossed.

When he spoke, his voice was deep and serious.

"A Wise One never resorts to cheap tricks like time machines and magic walking sticks. I am here to guide you back onto the road of Lucy, to help you find you. You lost your confidence, remember? That's the real purpose of our journey."

"But, don't you understand?" Lucy's voice had risen to a high, whiny pitch. "That will only happen if I can meet the artists so I can get an A!"

She looked at him suspiciously. "Are you sure you're a real Wise One or are you some sort of messenger taking me to my actual Wise One?"

Wilbur drew himself up to his full height, stretching his neck like an ostrich.

"I am the wisest of all the Wise Ones because I am the Guide and Lamplighter of the Moriels," said Wilbur, dignified and serious. "I will decide on which road you travel and that's an end to it."

"Wait," she said, puzzled, "You never mentioned Moriels. Who are the Moriels?" Wilbur's eyes brightened and the two little curly cues in the corners of his mouth squinched together. Evidently, this was one of his favorite subjects.

"The Moriels are beings whose only job is helping children, all kinds of children: bored children, sneaky children, sad children, spitting children, very naughty children, sticky children, lazy children, and lost children, like you."

"Do they all look like you?" Lucy asked.

"Gracious no," said Wilbur. "If I had thought you really and truly wanted some old wizard Wise One, I could have looked like one. But, aren't I much cuter and easier to talk to?"

Lucy did like him just as he was, but he wasn't all that easy to talk to because he never answered her exact questions.

"Yes," she said, "You're much cuter than an old wizard. Where do the Moriels live?"

"We live two universes away on a planet called Wilwahren. It means Garden of Ideas. We don't measure time; we just have fun. And, of course, our wavelengths are always listening for a child in trouble."

"Are we on Wilwahren now?" she asked.

"No, we are in another dimension, a place you and your friend Sam have talked about at length. You entered it the moment you jumped onto the red path."

"I knew it!" She said. "I just knew we were right about magic land. So, besides finding the road to Lucy, you will take me back to meet my artists?"

Wilbur grinned at her, wagging his rear end vigorously from side to side. His large ears flared out from his head like wings.

"Yes," he said. "I will also guide you to the artists on your list. Try not to be so impatient. You have so much to learn."

Lucy sighed with relief. "That's okay," she said. "I like learning."

They entered a dark glade of towering pine trees, where the only light came from blinking fireflies.

"What is this place?" she whispered in awe.

"We are right outside my garden," said Wilbur. He placed his paw on her wrist and guided her into another world.

Chapter 5

Wilbur's World

Wilbur led Lucy into an enchanted garden filled with flowers in every shade of blue. The sun was so bright that it gave the air diamond brilliance. After the dark woods, Lucy had to shade her eyes against the otherworldly light. They walked through trellises dripping with blue roses, past wishing wells sparkling with lucky crystals, and across lawns edged with curving beds of flowers. Wilbur untangled some irises growing around the base of a bird bath.

"There," he told them, "Feel better?"

The irises bowed their heads toward him. Wilbur stood admiring his garden with his paws clasped behind his back. He closed his eyes, breathed deeply, and, within seconds, his whole body glowed with a royal blue light. Lucy stared at him, absolutely flabbergasted.

"Wilbur, you're blue!" she cried. "How did you do that? Will you teach me?"

He turned his black-rimmed eyes on her and said, "When you learn to merge your essence with the essence of another living thing, you will both glow the same color. Smell your favorite flower. Breathe in its essence."

Lucy breathed in the lemony scent of a blue rose, but nothing happened.

"Give it time," said Wilbur. "Let's go see my house."

"You have an actual house?" She asked, surprised that a Wise One would live in something as regular as a plain old house.

"Of course, I have a house," he said. "Where would I keep all my medals and awards? I am quite famous, you know. I have saved ice planets from melting. I rescued the poor parallelograms from the beastly Blabbermouths, and I even sewed up a black hole or two. Oh! And there was that time I flicked on some chromatic aberrations, just for a second, you understand."

"*You* made a chromatic aberration?" Lucy asked, thinking about what Sam had said. "So, after you did all that, the people, or whatever were so grateful that they gave you medals and presents?"

"Truckloads of them," said Wilbur.

Now, they were walking on a narrow path, past water lily ponds. Propped up on hind legs that looked like springy shock absorbers, his furry behind wiggle-waggled from side to side.. As they approached Wilbur's house, Lucy thought about her own house and her parents. They would worry if she were not home for breakfast.

She touched his shoulder and said, "Wilbur, it's important for me to be home before my parents begin to worry. I don't want them to think I'm lost or kidnapped, or hurt."

Wilbur sat on his haunches with his tail in a neat curve around his feet and, breathing deeply, he pointed his face at the sun. His eyes were two merry slits, his smile wider and curlier than ever. Lucy could only imagine what disgusting smells he must be

34

inhaling: sour milk from a farm in Wales, rotten eggs from Timbuctoo, putrid manure from Australia, maybe even the droppings of some revolting alien creature from his planet. Wilbur sighed with pleasure and then it happened again. She watched his blue light brighten into a warm, golden yellow, glowing from his toes to his ears.

Is he ever going to answer me? She wondered.

"Mm," he said, "Doesn't that sun feel delicious?"

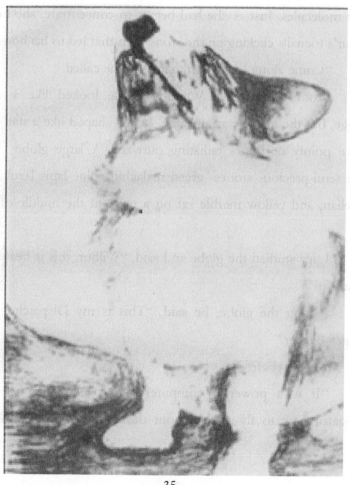

Glancing sideways at her, he said, "Let me take care of time-related problems. Your parents will not even know you are gone."

"Are you sure?"

"I guarantee it," he said.

Lucy said, "Please teach me to change colors. I have always wanted to see what I would look like with yellow hair."

She closed her eyes, letting the sun's warmth seep into her. Wilbur's merging essences idea reminded her of Sam's genius-laden molecules. Just as she had begun to concentrate, she heard Wilbur's toenails clicking on the stone path that led to his house.

"Come along Lucy, don't dawdle," he called.

From the outside, Wilbur's house looked like a cozy cottage, but the inside was amazing. It was shaped like a star with twelve pointy corridors radiating outward. A large globe made from semi-precious stones- green malachite, blue lapis lazuli, red carnelian, and yellow marble sat on a table in the middle of the star.

Lucy studied the globe and said, "Wilbur, this is beautiful. What is it?"

Patting the globe, he said, "This is my Dispatcher and Bringer-Backer."

"Your what?"

"It is a powerful computer. We need it to tell The Navigator how to fly safely to our destination. For example, if there happens to be a meteor shower up ahead, it will give the Navigator an alternate route."

Lucy was confused. "What's the Navigator?"

"Oh, you're going to love it. It's a small device that we'll take with us. I'll show you."

"But, wait a minute," said Lucy, confused. "You said Wise Ones never use trick gadgets."

"These are not tricks!" Wilbur said. "The Dispatcher is an expert communicator! It will power the Navigator's brain so that it will lead us to the right time and place. Give me a boost and I will show you how it works."

Lucy pushed his furry behind onto the table. He leaned over the top of the globe and chanted this odd phrase: "*Uctueam passus revolveraquem Quarkus Quackus.* The top of the globe spiraled open long enough for him to reach inside and lift out a round gadget.

"This is the Navigator," he said, proudly holding a small, round object aloft. Handing it to Lucy, he said, "Here, get the feel of it."

The Navigator felt like a living thing in her hands. It had a crystal dome on the top side and underneath through a pane of glass, there were the springs, gears, and bells. Attached to the outer rim were jeweled switches.

"It looks like a compass with beautiful switches," she said.

"The Navigator is much more than a compass," said Wilbur. "It is a priceless device that will guide our flight. I'll show you."

He twisted a ruby switch and an inky, star-crowded sky emerged out of the darkness under the dome.

Peering through the crystal dome, Lucy saw eight pink moons.

"Wow, pink moons. Awesome! I've never heard about pink moons."

"Indeed," said Wilbur, "They are the moons around my planet, Wilwahren."

He tapped the dome of the Navigator and the stars arranged themselves into constellations.

"Those don't look like earth constellations," said Lucy.

"You are right. Those are the stars in the sky around Wilwahren."

Wilbur scampered onto a silver sofa.

"Sit with me," he said, patting the place next to him. "I have to tell you something."

Lucy bounced down beside him and said, "Okay, what is it?"

His smile grew a little wobbly, almost apologetic.

"Well," he said, "There is one teeny thing that might cause a problem. I have never traveled back in earth time."

Lucy was speechless.

"But…but, these magic gadgets you invented for me will work, won't they?" She asked, nervously.

"Yes," he said, grabbing her hand, "Don't panic. They probably will work."

"What if something bad happens?" She asked.

"The Dispatcher, the Navigator, and I are all connected by our wavelengths. If they are tuned together, then they can send messages back and forth and the trip will be fine. When we're all tuned in, bright green light glows from us, but, if we even flicker another color, it means something is wrong."

"What would be wrong? These are powerful gadgets. You're magic and you made them." Lucy had always been a worrier and this was a big worry.

"Weell," he said. "If a virus infected the Navigator, first of all, it would break all communication. We would turn disgusting colors, and it could infect me as well."

Lucy jumped off the sofa. "You mean we could crash? Or you could get sick? Or we could be stuck in prehistoric times?" She shrieked.

Wilbur slid off the sofa too and stood on his short, sturdy legs looking up at her.

"Don't worry," he told her.

"Don't say 'don't worry,'" said Lucy. "Whenever grownups say 'don't worry,' it means there's something huge to worry about."

39

Then she remembered something else that he had said earlier.

"Wait a minute. What was that thing you said about our flight? You don't mean we're going to fly, as in fly, do you?"

Wilbur smiled his widest, happiest smile. Bobbing his head up and down, swinging his whole body from side to side, he said, "Yes! That's exactly what I mean. Isn't it exciting?"

Lucy looked stricken. "Not outside of an airplane?"

Wilbur clapped his paws. "Oh, Lucy, there is nothing as exhilarating as flying with the wind. You will never want to fly inside those rattle, old claptrap airplanes on earth again."

"Let me get this straight," she said. "You want me to flap my arms and fly?"

"Yup," said Wilbur. "Well, no, but flap away if it makes you happy. I manage beautifully without moving a muscle."

Lucy threw her arms in the air. "Haven't you ever heard of Newton? There's such a thing as gravity, you know."

Wilbur's voice was kind and steady when he spoke. "But, I've told you. We're in another dimension. You don't have to let things like gravity hold you back, not from flying, not from anything."

Lucy collapsed on the sofa.

Wilbur scrambled up beside her and dropped his head onto her shoulder, saying, "Trust me, Lucy I would never let anything hurt you."

His silky ear touched her cheek and his sweet, baby blanket smell calmed her.

"I do trust you," she said, stroking the wide space between his ears.

Before they left his house, Wilbur bustled around the room, straightening knick-knacks, hanging up a variety of jeweled belts with matching wands, and rotating the position of a ruby sleigh.

He said, "Lucy, give me that Flash Drive thingy. We can't take it with us."

Lucy lifted the ribbon with her Flash Drive attached to it over her head and handed it to him. He placed it carefully on the table near the Dispatcher.

"Now comes the real fun," Wilbur chuckled and skipped out the door.

Chapter 6

Wade Through the Liquid Mirrors and Fly!

It was already dark when Lucy joined Wilbur outside. Time seemed to move much faster in this world. He sat with his back to her talking to his garden.

"Wilbur, is someone out there?" She asked.

"Shush, they are timid."

"Who are they?"

He waved a foreleg in a wide circle, lighting the night air with thousands of twinkling colored lights

Wilbur blinked and Lucy saw a troupe of fairies dancing among the delphiniums and forget-me-nots. Their silver wings fluttered as they flew from petal to petal. They wore tiny flowers on their heads and carried colored lamps attached to the ends of rods.

"These are my gardeners," said Wilbur. "I was just telling them that the delphiniums need extra water this year."

"Their dresses have raggedy hems exactly like the material I saw last night floating in front of the moon." Lucy pointed to a violet fairy who was waving at Wilbur. "Was that her?"

Wilbur said, "My fairies are a great help with my children projects. Lilac is only too happy to run errands."

"You didn't answer my question again."

"No I didn't. Come with me."

Wilbur thrashed his way through a thicket of blueberry bushes until he came to an old potting shed. He stopped at the front door, mumbling and fumbling through his many fur pockets.

"Fiddlesticks! Where did I leave that key? I am always losing things."

"Ah-hah!" He shouted, holding up a gold key. "Here it is."

The door to the potting shed squeaked open, releasing the smells of damp earth, peat moss, and clay. Wilbur pulled the string attached to an overhead light and Lucy found herself in a small room with hundreds of colored bottles covering the walls, each one neatly corked and labelled. Wilbur unhooked a white apron and a pad and pencil from the wall. He tied the apron around his waist and fastened his spectacles behind his ears. Clenching the pad and pencil in his mouth, he climbed onto a Wilbur-size footstool and inspected the bottles. Lucy watched him lift one, peer at it over his glasses, mumble something, then replace it and move on.

"Are you looking for something specific?" She asked.

Wilbur was too busy to hear her. Then, with a great "Ah-ha, there you are," he plucked a blue bottle from the shelf.

Lucy craned her neck in order to read the label. It said, 'Throttle.'

He scribbled a notation on the pad and dropped the bottle into one of his endless supply of fur pockets. He resumed his searching and mumbling. Lucy heard him say something about whirlpools and crickets.

"These days, dipoles are jumping into whirlpool galaxies like crickets. It's not my fault if there are a few chromatic aberrations."

"What are you talking about?" Lucy asked.

He said, "I dearly hope this works."

"What?" She cried. "Now what are you talking about?"

"Not to worry. I'm an expert."

"An expert what?" Lucy said.

Wilbur ignored her and went on scanning the rows of bottles, tapping each one with a toenail. With another "Ah-ha," he plucked a silver bottle with 'Lift Off' on the label and dropped it into a fur pocket.

"Are you sure that's the right bottle?" she asked.

"If it's not, we're in for some rough sailing."

"Oh no," Lucy moaned. "Wilbur?"

"Mm-mm?" He said, swiveling his head in her direction with the pencil in his mouth.

"I'm a simple earth child and the idea of flying and what you said about dipoles, and all these bottles is making me nervous. I don't know what you're talking about. Can you please speak regular English?"

"Okeydokey," said Wilbur, taking off his apron and flicking off the overhead light.

He left the potting shed, Lucy following close behind, but after a few steps, Wilbur stopped so suddenly that she bumped into him.

"Sorry," he said, "I forgot something."

He hung a battered sign on the door of the potting shed. This was written on the sign: *There is absolutely nothing interesting in here.*

Lucy hurried after him through the thicket of blueberry bushes as they left the potting shed. Only the bell-like voices of Wilbur's fairy gardeners broke the silence of the night. Their glowing lamps left trails of blue, orange, yellow and pink light as they flew. Lucy followed Wilbur under an archway hung with blue roses as big as cabbages to the open lawn. She sat on a stone bench that had been plunked right in the middle of the purple irises.

"Sit down for a minute, Wilbur."

Wilbur climbed onto the bench and folded his paws.

"First of all," said Lucy. "I have to know exactly how you're going make us fly. Are you going to splash us with the stuff in those bottles or shoot us out of a cannon?"

She studied his solemn face. There was something so staunch and dependable about the way his large ears perked straight up that she would believe anything he told her.

"Gracious me, I do believe you are a born worrier," said Wilbur. "No one is getting splashed and I don't even own a cannon. They are way too bulky and besides, they are hollow."

"Of *course* they're hollow," said Lucy. "You say the strangest things. But, how are we going to fly? Did you do something scientific to make sure we don't fall down?"

45

Wilbur's eyes widened in surprise, he arched his brow, and his ears stuck straight out on either side of his head.

"Is that all you are worried about?" He said. "Of course I did something. I flattened our thoughts into wavelengths. Then I put them onto parallel computers, which implemented the time-warp mechanism."

Lucy looked at him suspiciously. Was it even possible to flatten thoughts into wave lengths?

"Flatten out wavelengths," she repeated. "That's going to make us fly?"

"No," said Wilbur, "That fixes the time travel problem. Time travel is only a question of flattening and expanding energy. And you have enough energy in your head to take us to Jupiter."

Lucy held her head in her hands. She felt like screaming. He still had not told her specifically how they were going to fly.

"But how are we going to get up in the air and move through it?" She shouted.

Wilbur was marching toward a strip of grass when he turned around and said, "Easy, we are going to use the liquid mirrors in the bottles you watched me choose. Liquid mirrors give the novice levitator a tremendous boost."

Wide-eyed and doubtful, she said, "Liquid mirrors? But how can a mirror…"

"This is the launching pad," interrupted Wilbur, as they came to a strip of grass lined by a picket fence.

Lucy watched him produce two silver bowls from his pockets and lay them on the launching pad. Then he took the blue and silver bottles from his pockets and he poured the contents into each bowl.

"There," he said, proudly. "Our liquid mirrors."

The wobbly gobbledygook looked like Jell-O. Lucy watched the liquid began to spin, whirling faster and faster until she thought it might spin off into outer space.

"Hurry," said Wilbur. "We have no time to lose. Follow me!"

He hopped in and out of the bowls. His short, sturdy legs lifted off the ground together. He hung in the air suspended about twelve feet over Lucy's head.

"Make it snappy, Lucy," he barked. "Step into the bowls."

Lucy waded into one bowl and then the next. Just as her foot lifted out of the second bowl, there was a terrific flash of light. The launching pad flapped like a silky green sheet enveloping her for a second. Then, the magic happened. She felt her feet lift off the ground and her whole self rise up to where Wilbur was waiting for her. Oh that feeling! The feeling of something wonderful swooping through your insides was like nothing else Lucy had ever felt. It was as if every part of her was giggling, especially her heart. She had never in her life experienced anything like the joy of that moment.

They flew on the wind through the starry sky. Lucy's red hair streamed behind her gleaming in the moonlight. Wilbur flew right beside her, his large, pointy ears blown back on his head and his smile so big that his pink tongue hung out of his mouth. His blue eye twinkled and his fur sparkled like green stardust. With his front and back legs extended all the way out, he looked exactly like a miniature superman.

Lucy flew close to him, nuzzling his snowy mane.

"I love you, Wilbur. This is the happiest moment of my life."

He patted her hand with his paw and said, "You are a gifted, loving child, and you're safe with me. Appreciate the here and now. The memories of this journey will stay in your heart for the rest of your life."

Lucy felt the warm, salty air of the ocean on her face. Passing a cluster of bright stars, Lucy thought she smelled honey.

"Do you smell honey, Wilbur?"

"Those are the Pleiades," he said, happily. "They are star sisters and the honey gatherers of your universe."

Night faded and the pink and silver ribbons of dawn spread across the horizon.

"Look, Wilbur," Lucy cried, pointing ahead. "Daylight!"

Chapter 7

Jumping Into Springtime

Lucy and Wilbur reached the poppy-spangled hills outside Florence, Italy on a warm April day in the year 1480. The sun looked like a silver coin scorching the blue sky. They descended slowly over a poppy field, swinging back and forth like a pendulum. Wilbur landed on all four paws, swallowed up completely by the tall wildflowers. Waist high amidst the tall flowers, Lucy looked around for him but he was nowhere to be seen.

"Wilbur?" She called, nervously.

"I'm over here," said a small voice.

Peering through the flowers, Lucy spotted a black nose and one blue eye.

"I can hardly see you," she said.

"That's not surprising. Pick me up, please," he said.

"Why don't you just fly up?" She said, inches from his face.

Wilbur held her gaze with serious eyes.

"Because," he said, "magic is too big to be used for small things. Remember that."

Lucy picked him up. His barrel-shaped body was warm and soft. Holding him close, feeling the thump of his little heart, and breathing his sweet smell, made her feel happy and safe.

"Put me down over there near the olive grove, please."

High above the glimmering city of Florence, in the shade of the silver-leafed olive trees, Wilbur told Lucy about the artist whom they would visit first.

"The fifteenth century was a time of great artistic achievement," he said. "It is called the Renaissance. Three artists on your list lived here at different times. Don't worry, you will meet all three. While we're here, I have to pretend to be your pet dog."

Lucy looked horrified. "But, that's not dignified. You can't be owned by anyone."

"No," he said, "But, very few people know that. Also, you take the Navigator." Handing it to her, he said. "Okey dokey, it's time to go."

Lucy looked down at her blue dress and silver boots.

"But, what about...?"

"Uh-oh," said Wilbur, looking dubiously at Lucy's clothes. "You're right. Those clothes will shock these fifteenth-century people out of their wits."

He blinked, transforming Lucy's clothes into a long, red velvet dress with tight, gold embroidered sleeves and a flat, round cap sewn with tiny pearls.

"Wow!" She said, running her fingers over the velvet pleats, "You're just like a fairy godmother. Can I keep these things?"

Wilbur shook his head. "Sorry, nothing leaves the wardrobe. Let's go meet Sandro Botticelli, the first artist. He is just finishing a very large painting of *Springtime*."

They walked down one of the steep cobblestone paths into the city of Florence. Lucy stared, awestruck at the color and activity in the narrow street they entered. Clowns doing back flips, musicians playing mandolins, and teenage boys and girls jostled alongside men and women in fancy clothes. The women wore heavy, brocade dresses laced up the back and the men wore tights, velvet jackets, and hats with long white feathers.

"I can't believe the men actually wear tights," said Lucy, giggling.

"Don't gawk," said Wilbur, "Just smile and walk with your head up and, for heaven's sake, don't step on any monkeys. They are very popular here."

Wilbur walked at a fast clip so that she had to run ahead and shuffle backwards in front of him. "Can I get a necklace or a notebook and a pen so I can take notes?"

"No jewelry and definitely no notes," said Wilbur, sternly. "You have plenty of knowledge. Now, it's time to understand. You will learn much better if you look and listen."

"That's no fun," she said.

"Nope, it isn't. But, look at it this way, next time you visit Florence, you can buy as many diamond crowns and as much paper as you can get through Customs."

51

"How do you know about Customs?" Lucy said, surprised that Wilbur knew about an inconvenience like Customs.

"I told you," he said, "I know everything that is important. By the way, never, ever use an anomaly."

"What's an *amonaly*?" Lucy asked.

"A-nom-aly," said Wilbur. "It means something that is out of context. For example, Edison hasn't been born yet so, if you said, 'Turn on the electric lights,' all the atmospheric windows would forget to close."

"Is that bad?" Lucy asked.

"Well, it's not good." said Wilbur.

The Navigator directed them to a quiet square with a lovely orange house decorated with garlands of fruit and flowers.

"This is Sandro's house," said Wilbur. "Knock on the door."

Wilbur sat on the front stoop waving at passersby. A butler, who looked like a snobby pig, opened the heavy wooden door.

Lucy said, "Please tell Sandro that Lucy Nightingale would like to visit him."

The butler bowed, and said, "Just a moment, young lady. Come in, but leave your mutt outside."

Lucy was furious. "He is not a mutt," she said, "not only that, he's not *my* mutt. Dogs don't belong to people, they live with them."

Wilbur gave the grumpy butler his sweetest smile and followed Lucy inside.

He lowered his voice and said, "Don't try to teach them anything. Grownup minds are too schmuckered up with worries about the lawn and taxes to understand."

A handsome, young man wearing red tights, a white shirt with billowing sleeves and lace cuffs, and a red velvet jacket pattered down the stairs.

The man kissed Lucy's hand. "I am Sandro, and you must be Lucy."

"Yes, I am. I saw one of your beautiful paintings, and I would be so grateful if you would show me more."

"That's a nice compliment," said the artist. "Yes, of course, I will show you what I have just finished painting today." Sandro looked at Wilbur and smiled. "What a nice doggie."

Lucy patted Wilbur's head and said, "This is Wilbur. He gets very upset if he's not with me every minute."

"Well then, Wilbur," said Sandro. "Please come with us."

Sandro took the stairs two at a time, leading them down corridors hung with pink and green chandeliers and silk wall hangings, and finally he ushered them into a large, sunny room. Glass jars covered the tables: jars filled with colored powders, jars crammed full with brushes, and jars filled with oil. Wilbur curled up in a corner and picked up a book about what fifteenth-century dogs liked to eat.

"This is my studio, where I paint," said Sandro.

Nine six foot high panels, hinged together like a screen, stood against the far wall. Lucy had a copy of this very painting in her bedroom, but that was a small, dull picture. The work of art in front of her opened up a fantasy world, a garden of beautiful goddesses, orange trees, and flowers, where colors sparkled like jewels.

"This is like looking at a beautiful fairy world," she said in a whispery voice.

"Yes," said Sandro, "I think it is one of my masterpieces."

Pink and red roses, purple violets, blue bells, and white crocuses covered a meadow of dark green grass. A golden haired goddess, wearing a crown of flowers and a dress covered with roses, walked toward Lucy as if she might step out of the painting into the room. Other gods and goddesses danced, flew, or floated around her. Slender trees, hung with oranges and white flowers grew behind them.

Lucy looked up at Sandro, and said, "The colors are probably so bright because you're such a happy man."

What had she just said? She realized that she had just answered the first question of her assignment. Sandro's happy personality showed in his bright colors and his energetic figures.

"You are right," said Sandro. "I never thought about it."

"It's a wonderful painting," said Lucy. "I'm sure lots of people will want to buy it."

"It has already been sold to a rich banker named Lorenzo the Magnificent. He is giving it to his nephew's bride as a wedding present. Hey, I just had an idea. Would you like to come with me to the wedding reception this afternoon?" Sandro said.

Lucy nodded, but she was studying the oranges that hung from slender trees in the background.

"Those oranges are awfully big compared with the spindly trees. Does it mean something?"

"Do you know what 'coat of arms' is?" Sandro asked.

"I think so," said Lucy. "Isn't it a family shield with a picture on it?"

"Yes it is. Each family in Florence has a different coat of arms. Lorenzo wanted everyone who sees this painting to know that it was his present to the bride. His coat of arms is five orange balls, which are symbolized by the oranges in the trees."

"That is so amazing. It's a hidden secret in the painting, telling everyone how rich and generous he is." Lucy said.

"What do you like best about the painting, Lucy?"

"Well, first I love that it's almost as big as the whole wall. It makes me want to walk into it. And, then I love the flowers and colors, but my favorite person in the painting is the smiling lady with the beautiful long, blond hair sprinkling roses on the grass. Who is she?"

"She is called Flora, the goddess of spring," said Sandro. "Touch the flowers on her dress."

Lucy ran her hand over the bumpy plants on Flora's dress.

"Wow," she said, "They're actually lumpy just like real roses and it's the flower, the stem, and even the roots. That's so cool."

Lucy noticed something in the painting that did not make sense.

"I have a question," said Lucy. "See how Flora's feet don't really touch the ground and her dress is all fluttery, like the wind is blowing it?"

"Yes, I see," said Sandro.

"Okay, now look at the lady in the middle," she said, pointing to the woman on Flora's right side.

Sandro' eyes slid back to the figure in the middle of the painting.

"Yes?" Sandro said.

"She's not floating at all. You can see that she's standing on the ground. Not only that, if the wind is blowing Flora's dress, why isn't it blowing that woman's dress?"

Sandro smacked his forehead. "Holy octopuses! You are smart."

"So why did you make the middle woman so different?"

"She is different because she is not a goddess. She is a portrait of the bride wearing a white wedding dress."

"Then where is her coat of arms?" Lucy asked

"Now that you mention it, I did not put it in."

"Don't you think you should?" Lucy asked. "You put the oranges in the painting to stand for Lorenzo's coat of arms so shouldn't you hide the bride's coat of arms somewhere in the painting too?"

Sandro said, "You are absolutely right. Besides, I love putting hidden messages in my paintings. I am going to whip up some gold paint and give her a necklace with a crescent moon, her family's coat of arms."

He sprinkled some gold powder onto his palette and a drop of oil and mixed them together into smooth gold paint. He chose a brush and painted a crescent moon hung from a delicate gold chain around the bride's neck.

"There, Lucy, now you are part creator of my painting."

He actually painted my idea, thought Lucy.

She felt like as if she might burst with happiness. She felt like dancing around the room.

"It's a wonderful painting. I'm sure lots of people would want to buy it," said Lucy.

Just then, the church bells rang three times.

"We have to leave for the wedding reception. My friend is delivering the painting to the bride's house in a few minutes."

Wilbur's book had put him to sleep. As they left the room, Sandro said, "Wake up, little Wilbur. We are going to a party."

Chapter 8

Escape

The wedding reception took place in a grand palace, overlooking the Arno River. There were lemon trees in clay pots in front of a massive door. Sandro, Lucy, and Wilbur walked into a hallway painted with garlands of flowers. Raucous laughter, hooting, honking, clinking glasses, and music drifted from the room next door. The bride and groom sat at a long table talking to their friends, while jugglers and musicians performed in front of them. Jewels flashed in the dim candle light. Shadows danced on the walls. The smoke from the candles of a massive iron chandelier and the torches attached to the walls stung Lucy's eyes.

Sandro pushed his way through the crowd, occasionally greeting his fans. However, poor Wilbur, who detested crowded spaces because he suffered from claustrophobia, was a nervous wreck. He maneuvered as best he could through the forest of knobby legs and dresses as heavy as curtains.

In a trembling voice he said, "We must be ready for anything."

"Like what?" Lucy said, looking around, nervously.

"Like falling torches, flying drumsticks, goblets, large spatulas, and other rotisserie items," said Wilbur.

Lucy quickly picked Wilbur up to protect him.

"I am neither feeble, nor helpless," he said in her ear. "However, thank you for lifting me from that tangle of smelly

59

feet. Try not to worry so much about me. Appreciate the here and now."

"I am!" She said. "I can appreciate more than one thing at a time, you know."

They hurried after Sandro until at last they reached the end wall of the room. It was quieter there and less crowded. Setting Wilbur down gently on the stone floor, Lucy looked around and felt as if she had walking into the fanciest jewelry shop in the world. The bride's dazzling wedding presents covered every surface. There were gleaming gold and silver goblets, glittering jewels, yards of milky white pearls, painted china, enameled tiles, and, of course, Sandro's exquisite painting, which hung in all its glory on the wall. Lucy made a bee line for the jewelry.

"Wow, the bride is lucky to have all this jewelry," she said, decking herself out in ruby and sapphire rings, pearls, and a diamond tiara.

Wilbur whispered, "Put those baubles back immediately! Someone is bound to come and haul you off to a most unpleasant prison."

Lucy did as she was told just in time. Growling and heavy footsteps were pounding the floor in their direction. Sandro was so immersed in admiring his painting that he was not listening. After all, he had nothing to fear from anyone. He was an honored guest. On the other hand, Lucy and Wilbur could be regarded as guilty party crashers. It was too late to hide so they stood at attention trying to look innocent.

The footsteps and growling belonged to a huge, red-faced ogress who stood in the doorway, carrying a rolling pin in one scaly hand and a carving knife in the other. *That's the messiest person I've ever seen,* thought Lucy. *She's probably the cook.* The woman's grey hair stuck out like crooked wires from under a silly, frilly cap. She only had four teeth. There were ugly hairs sprouting from a wart on her chin. One of her eyes looked dead and the other one bulged out of its socket. All in all, she was extremely revolting. The most extraordinary thing was that this scary woman reminded Lucy of Miss Dawson. Lucy couldn't help thinking of Miss Dawson's ruler as she stared at this woman's long, sharp, shiny knife.

"She looks like Miss Dawson's fat sister," yelped Lucy.

"You know this creature?" Wilbur said.

"Not exactly," said Lucy. "But she looks just like my horrible teacher, only she's huge and she has a knife instead of a ruler."

At the sight of Lucy and Wilbur, the ogress' flabby lips twisted into a snarly knot, revealing her yellow teeth. Her bulging, good eye slid like a marble from Lucy to Wilbur.

"Uh-oh," said Wilbur, "We might be goners."

Two meaty hands lunged for him but he scurried under a table.

"Dirty mutt, yew should be locked up with the other beasts," the cook screeched.

61

She squinted at Lucy and growled, "Arrghh, as for yew, Grizzelelda, you're the new scullery maid so why aren't you in the kitchen scullerering and stirring the banana pudding?"

"Who's Grizzlelda?" Lucy yelled. "Let go of me, you horrible person, whatever your name is."

"Gobble, Gobble! My name is Gobble, you dummy," she hollered. "And I'm going to boil you up for stew if you don't get back to that stirring."

"You've got me mixed up with someone else," said Lucy, trying to wrench free of Gobble's lethal grip.

"It was you, Stupid Head. "Five minutes ago I put a spoon in yer hand to stir the pudding and now I find you with a mutt pretending to be a guest."

"I never had a spoon," Lucy yelled. "And I'm not pretending to be a guest. I am a guest!"

Meanwhile, Wilbur was jumping up and down on all four legs, barking furiously at the cook.

"I hate mongrels!" She bellowed, letting go of Lucy and lunging for Wilbur.

Lucy pinched Gobble, shouting, "Leave him alone. He's innocent. Go scrub a floor or something?"

But, Gobble grabbed Wilbur around the middle and hauled him away.

"Bite her, Wilbur!" Lucy screamed.

"I can't. Her arms are too stubby," he said.

Lucy followed them through the dining area where the air was thick and pasty, and filled with the disgusting smells of a roasting pig and boiling cabbage. Wilbur wriggled out of Gobble's arms and fell on the floor. The cook grabbed a broom stick and poked him with it. Wilbur's paws skittered across the stone floor, as she poked him into a pen, occupied by two pigs, three sheep, and a family of ducks. Before, the cook dragged her away, Lucy heard Wilbur greeting the animals in the pen.

"Good evening, fellow hostages."

Gobble put both of her red hands on Lucy's shoulders and twisted her in the direction of the kitchen, jabbing her in the back with a warty finger.

"Back to the pudding stirring for yew, Grizzelelda and no more back talk."

With each poke, Lucy felt the Navigator bounce wildly in her pocket. The kitchen looked like a cave, stone walls, a few tables, and a cauldron hung over huge fire place. *That huge cauldron must contain the famous banana pudding*, thought Lucy.

Then, the cook gave Lucy such a powerful shove that the Navigator flew out of her pocket, looped high in the air, and fell into the pot of pudding with a loud plop.

"Oh no!" Lucy gasped, horrified at the possibility of losing it.

"What was that noise?" Gobble yelled, wheeling around and glaring at Lucy with her red eyeball.

"It was nothing. I just stubbed my toe," said Lucy, meekly.

If she could only get this horrid woman out of the way for a minute, she could rescue the Navigator from the disgusting pudding and save Wilbur.

Gobble plunked herself down onto a wooden bucket and fanned her red face with a paddle. Lucy hummed a lullaby, casting dopey smiles at the cook, as she stirred the pudding. Gobble's eyes rolled back in her head, the carving knife fell from her lap, and with a grunt that sounded like 'oink,' she dozed off.

In a flash, Lucy reached into the sticky pudding, grabbed the Navigator, and scampered around the corner to look for Wilbur. There was no time to lose. She had to find him to escape that insane, knife-wielding cook. *Poor Wilbur,* she thought, *if he's imprisoned, his claustrophobia will act up. He's probably wretched.* However, she was surprised to find Wilbur entertaining the other prisoners, happily recounting a long tale about his adventures with some creatures called the Perpendiculars.

He spotted her and smiled. "Ah, Lucy, there you are," he said. "Join us. I have just rung for some tea."

"Tea?" She screeched, unlocking the pen and grabbing his tail, "Have you gone crazy? There's a hairy cook with a carving knife coming for us!"

"Have you got the Navigator?" Wilbur said, standing up.

"I have it," she said, patting her pocket, "But it fell into a pot of the wedding glop. We have to clean it off right away so it doesn't get a virus."

"Later," said Wilbur. "Right now, we have to disappear."

"But how?" Lucy cried. "That awful woman has probably called the police or the army or whatever to capture us and burn us at the stake."

"I have a plan," said Wilbur. "Follow me, there's not a moment to lose."

They dashed back through the dining area, to the end of the room where Sandro's painting hung. Wilbur blinked and Lucy watched as something miraculous happened. The painting expanded in all directions. It pushed backwards through the wall of the room, and it grew sideways so that one whole wall became Sandro's garden. Even more magical, like a veil had been whisked off the painted surface, his meadow came to life. The enchanted garden of flowers imagined by Sandro was real. Lucy stood close to the line separating the stone floor of the fifteenth-century room and the grassy meadow. She closed her eyes for a second to feel the warm breeze wafting from the meadow into the room. Wilbur jolted her out of her daydream.

"Jump!" He shouted.

They leapt from the stone floor of the room and landed on the spongy grass of the garden. As she leapt from one world into another, the opening to that other world, the world of the fifteenth-century bride, had shut forever. Standing in Sandro's meadow, she turned around and looked back at the noisy wedding party. She felt as if she were looking through an invisible window at another world, only it was the frozen, silent world of a painting. The wedding party had become a painting with the bride and groom sitting at a long table watching jugglers and musicians. The room was full of people wearing rich fabrics and sparkling jewels. Among the crowd of laughing guests, one face looked directly at her. It was Sandro and he was smiling. In the lower corner of the foreground, Gobble, her face as angry and as red as a beet, knelt on all fours scrubbing the black and white marble floor.

Lucy turned away from the painted world. She knelt beside Wilbur and looked at the bright, exciting world they had just entered. The grass was dotted with hundreds of blooming flowers. She combed her fingers through the dark blades, lilac crocuses and blue hyacinths. The floating goddesses towered over her and little Wilbur. Lucy looked up at Flora's beautiful, smiling face and her long golden hair. Maybe it was her dreamy smile or the way she floated above the ground, but Flora reminded Lucy of Miss Lang.

"She looks like my new teacher," Lucy whispered to Wilbur.

"Believe me," he said, "she is most certainly not your teacher."

Lucy yelped and nearly fell on top of Wilbur when Flora groaned and dropped her armful of flowers. Even more frightening, her large blue eyes slid in Lucy's direction and she actually spoke.

"I guess I should thank you for trespassing in my meadow because now I can stop smiling and I can drop all these flowers. They're absolutely crawling with bugs. Who are you anyway?"

66

Lucy whispered, "Did you see that, Wilbur? That painted goddess dropped all her things and spoke to me."

"Yes," said Wilbur. "She's real now. I think you and Sandro are a lot alike. Your thoughts are strong enough to make things come alive."

"Hey, you, little girl over there," said Flora, "Where are you?" Flora strained to look behind her, but it was no use. Sandro had painted her facing forward and she could not turn her head.

"I'm here," said Lucy, walking around in front of her.

Flora looked at Lucy's long red hair and rumpled dress and said, "I can't imagine who let you into my picnic garden."

"Nobody let us in. We just jumped to get away from a horrible cook."

"Jumped? What is 'jumped?' It doesn't sound very dainty. I never do anything undainty. As you can see, I am so beautiful that I can float and skip and throw roses all over the place. Are there more of you in here?" She said, trying desperately to look behind her.

Lucy said, "There is me and my wonderful friend, Wilbur."

"Who is this Wilbur?" Flora asked, frowning. "He better be clean. Bring him over here so I can inspect him."

Lucy called to Wilbur, "Come over and meet her highness, Flora."

Wilbur trotted jauntily in front of Flora. He was on his best behavior, his ears were their perkiest and his smile was its curviest.

"Hello," he said. "My, that's a lovely flower arrangement you have around your neck."

Flora took one look at Wilbur, gathered up her skirts, and screeched, "Eek, a horrid bork!"

Her flower crown slipped down in front of her eyes and her hair flew out like a scarecrow.

Glaring at Lucy, she said, "How dare you ruin my picnic garden with a revolting bork?"

Lucy glared right back at Flora.

"He is not a bork. For all I know, you could be a bork."

Flora's face crumpled up like a squashed pie.

"We need to get out of here before that madwoman smears all the paint on Sandro's masterpiece," Wilbur said.

Lucy nodded and they wound their way through the orange trees, leaving Sandro's painted world forever.

Chapter 9

Mr. Genius

Lucy and Wilbur emerged from Sandro's orange grove into one of the crowded streets leading to Florence's main square. The Navigator tugged at her pocket like a heavy wet stone. She hoped that the pudding had not broken its wavelengths. Wilbur had told her that the Navigator could get a virus. Did that mean Wilbur could also get a virus? She was not sure. All she knew was that she would have to watch him carefully.

"You have to look at the Navigator now," she told Wilbur. "I'm afraid that horrible banana slop got inside it."

Sidestepping the crowds, they ducked into an alley where Lucy pulled the Navigator from her pocket. It looked useless and forlorn. Bouncing around in Lucy's pocket had smeared its dome with the sticky pudding blotting out the map with its diamond trail. It was so thickly caked and dried around the jeweled switches that they would not move.

Wilbur's smile did not hide his solemn expression, even he was worried.

He said, "Clean it off as much as you can, Lucy. Rinse it with water from the drinking fountain over there."

She used her dress to scrape off as much pudding as she could and rinsed it until it looked clean. From now on, she would carry it in her hand or in the clean pocket.

"You better clean off your dress too," he said, "And hurry, we have to be at the town square in ten minutes on the dot."

He trotted off down the street, leaving her as she rinsed yellow goo from her dress. Wilbur's smallness made it easy for him to weave through the forest of legs. Lucy had to watch out for flying acrobats. She had to dodge back flipping clowns, and skirt around squealing children. Wilbur was waiting for her at the end of the street, leaning against a building and reading the *Florence Gazette*.

"My, my, you are slow and why do you look so grumpy?" He asked.

"For one thing," she said, "I got bumped and stepped on by clowns, monkeys, and someone who looked like a monk. And, for another thing, this dress is hot and scratchy and sticky."

"How about some Italian *gelato*, that's ice cream?" Wilbur suggested. "They make the most scrumptious ice cream in the world here."

"No thanks," she said. "What I'd really like is a tee shirt and some shorts. Do you have something else I could wear?"

Wilbur hauled a red Santa Claus type sack out of his hundreds of fur pockets.

"Let's see," he said, burying his head in the sack, "I have an extremely fashionable scuba diving suit. It has gills and fins. The fish will think you're one of them and they'll wave at you."

"No thanks," said Lucy. "I'd rather wear this dress than flip flop down the street looking like a huge fish. Do you have anything else?"

Wilbur stuck his head deeper into the bag. "Oh! Here's a lovely ermine costume you might like," he said, pulling out an ermine suit. It had a pointy face, a hideous, pointed nose, long whiskers, bony claws, and rat-like ears.

"Put that horrible thing away," said Lucy. "It looks like a scary possum. Never mind, I'll wear the dress."

Wilbur pointed to the open square ahead of them and said, "When we leave this street and enter the square, we will be passing through another one of the invisible curtains that separate time. And ten years will have passed since you met Sandro."

As they left the street, Lucy felt something brush across her eyes. This time she knew it was not cobwebs. Shimmering heat waves rose from the largest open square in Florence. Bewildered by the color and sounds around her, Lucy reached for Wilbur's paw. Water splashed from the spouts of four huge fountains. Women walked arm in arm, their silk and velvet dresses swishing across the cobblestones. Actors dressed all in gold, even their faces were painted gold, performed an opera. Along the edge of the square, vendors stood by open tents shouting their wares. Lucy was tempted to browse through colorful paper, leather pouches, gold necklaces, and summer clothes, but something caught her eye. Across the square, a man in a long coat was hauling a cart full of caged birds. Their frantic squawking sounded like cries for help.

"I'm going to find out what that man is going to do with all those birds," Lucy told Wilbur. Before he could answer her, she was halfway across the square. She caught up with the man as he was turning onto a steep alley.

"Excuse me, sir?" She said.

The man set the cart down and said, "Yes?"

His kind face and penetrating eyes surprised her. She expected a bird murderer to look like a scary monster. This man seemed kind and gentle.

"What is your name, child?" He asked.

"My name is Lucy Nightingale. I'm visiting Florence for the day. I saw you pulling all those birds away and I thought …" said Lucy.

Before she had a chance to finish, the man bowed, kissed her hand, and introduced himself.

"It is an honor to meet you, Lucy. I am called Leonardo da Vinci di Piero, which means that I am Leonardo, son of Peter from the town of Vinci."

Lucy gulped. *Way to go, Lucy,* she thought to herself. *You almost accused one of the greatest geniuses of all time of murder.* She needed Wilbur's help.

Looking nervously around for him, she told the man, "Excuse me, could you please wait a minute while I find my dog?"

Leonardo said, "Of course, I'll tell my birds a joke."

"Wilbur!" She shouted.

In less than a second, Wilbur appeared trotting across the square. He was balancing a dish of *gelato* on his nose. He slid the dish onto the ground and lapped it up with loud smacking sounds.

Leonardo had turned his attention to his birds so Lucy could speak to Wilbur privately.

Finishing off the last drop of gelato, Wilbur said, "Well, what can I do for you?"

"Do you know who this man is?" Lucy hissed under her breath.

Wilbur gave her a silly smile. The ice cream had made him sleepy.

"No?" Lucy said. "Well I'll tell you who he is. It's the actual Leonardo da Vinci. I chased the actual Leonardo da Vinci across the square and almost accused him of murdering those birds."

"Don't worry about it," said Wilbur. "Leonardo knows he's a genius so he takes everything as a compliment."

"That's a relief," said Lucy. She turned around to speak to the artist, but he was having a conversation with a parrot about bird seeds.

"Sorry to interrupt you," she said.

Leonardo gave her a brilliant smile and said, "I see your dog found you."

"Yes, I guess he did. His name is Wilbur."

Leonardo bent over and looked deep into Wilbur's eyes. "Yes, I know. Hello, my friend, you are a long way from home."

Wilbur wagged his tail.

"Mr. da Vinci," Lucy said, "do you have time to talk about art with me?"

"I would be honored. Please, call me Leonardo. You see 'da Vinci' is not my name. It is the town where I live."

"Oh, okay," said Lucy. "Are you taking those birds home with you?"

"No, not to my home; I am taking them back to their homes. Every Sunday, I buy up all the caged birds in the market and set them free. Do you want to help?"

"That would be fun," she said.

Leonardo and Lucy pulled the squeaky handcart up the alley toward the countryside.

"Wilbur?" Lucy called.

Wilbur was lagging behind. "I am feeling a little tired," he said. "I will ride on the back."

Lucy lifted him on to the end of the cart. Her heart clenched when she saw that his green glow was not as bright. *Virus?* She thought. *No, please don't let him be sick.*

He sat on the end of the handcart, as Lucy and Leonardo dragged it into an olive grove in the countryside outside of Florence. One by one, they opened the cages and the birds flew into the air. Freeing the birds reminded Lucy of releasing her butterfly wish. Now, she was living her wish. She shaded her eyes and watched the birds fly around in circles.

"They're looking for their families," she said.

By the time all the bird families had found each other, it was late afternoon.

"I have an important appointment at my studio this evening and must return to Vinci at once," said Leonardo. "Would you like to see my studio?'

"I'd love to," said Lucy.

It was almost twilight when they arrived at Leonardo's modest house in the village of Vinci. The artist ushered them into his studio. Wilbur scurried into a corner of the room and made himself comfortable on a cushion. The wonderful sights inside Leonardo's studio took Lucy by surprise. A flying machine with huge canvas wings swung from strings attached to the ceiling. There were miniature stages and water-powered clocks, merry-go-

75

rounds and a helicopter. A round capsule with a cork screw propeller attached to the top that looked like a space ship sat in one corner of the room. Sketchbooks lay open on Leonardo's desk. Ink drawings of the tiniest parts of a bird's wing bone structure and feathers, and written notes about how they moved on the currents of the wind-covered the pages.

"You really love birds?" Lucy said.

"When I was a little boy, I dreamed that one day I would invent a way to fly like a hawk," said Leonardo.

I know exactly how he feels, she thought.

He pointed to a winged structure that hung from the ceiling like a giant bat.

"After studying the mechanics of how birds fly, I built a flying machine for a human being. There is a seat and rudder to steer with between the wings."

"I wish I had time to try it."

She picked up one of the sketchbooks and stared at his handwriting.

"I don't mean to be rude, but is something wrong with your handwriting?"

Leonardo smiled at her and said, "It's easier for me to write backward and compose sentences from right to left. It looks crazy, but you can read it if you hold it up to a looking glass."

"Backwards writing," she said, amazed. His writing was backwards just like the shadows of her crystals. *That's a coincidence,* she thought. *Maybe backwards things aren't so bad.*

76

Leonardo guided her to an easel.

"I am working on a portrait of a young lady. Would you like to see it before she gets here?"

"Definitely," said Lucy. "Who is the woman?"

"She is the wife of a wealthy silk merchant called Giacondo. He hired me to paint an extraordinary portrait of his wife."

Leonardo whipped the canvas cover off the portrait. Lucy was face to face with the unfinished *Mona Lisa.*

She had seen the painting in reproductions, but the original was completely different. For one thing, it was quite small and for another, the colors were brighter. A young woman wearing an emerald green dress and delicate veil sat on a balcony that overlooked a misty landscape with paths, streams, and even snow-capped mountains.

"What's the title?" Lucy asked.

"Out of respect for Lisa's married status, I will call it Lady Lisa, or *Mona Lisa*," said Leonardo. "Lisa is fun-loving, even a bit naughty, and she is very much in love with her husband."

"The landscape behind her is spooky and mysterious," said Lucy. Where is it?"

"I made it up," said Leonardo, tapping his head. "An artist can invent anything he wants. I could even paint you and Wilbur wandering in the background of this portrait."

"How do you make those soft shadows in her face?" She asked.

"I paint portraits by candlelight because it creates beautiful shadows, soft edges, and mystery. Here, let me show you."

Leonardo lit an enormous candlestick and pulled up a stool for Lucy. He closed her hand around a brush and covered it with his own and guided her hand to the palette. When the brush was loaded with paint, together they swept a thin line of pale grey paint in the corner of Lisa's mouth. As if by magic, the shadow on the right side of her mouth created the impression of an upward curve.

"Wow," said Lucy. "I can't believe I just helped paint part of the *Mona Lisa*."

"You said this painting will be extraordinary, why?"

Leonardo sat on his painter's stool and said, "Stand behind me and look over my shoulder. Lisa is looking directly into my eyes so she will also look into the eyes of anyone who sees this painting and her eyes will follow you no matter where you move."

Lucy walked around the room. It was true; Lisa's eyes remained locked onto hers.

"That is unbelievably awesome," she said.

"No painter has ever done it before," said Leonardo. "I believe that the purpose of a portrait is to show a person's soul and the eyes are the windows to the soul."

The front door burst open and a dark-haired girl skipped into the studio.

"Hello," she said to Lucy, pouring herself a goblet of lemonade, "You must be a student. I'm Lisa and I'm sitting for that portrait."

She waved to Leonardo.

"Good evening, Mr. Genius. I saw you hauling your cart of birds this morning. You know you're too old for that. Your apprentices ought to do that sort of thing."

Leonardo sighed and pinched the bridge of his nose.

"I am as strong as an ox, thank you very much. Let me worry about my age and strength and you worry about smiling properly."

Lisa looked somewhat disappointed at the sight of the painting. "It's very gloomy. Couldn't you paint me dancing in a meadow picking pretty flowers?"

"No I could not," said Leonardo. "I am painting the real you, not some silly nymph in the forest. Trust me, Lisa this painting will be the hit of the year. Now, go sit down, turn your head slightly to your left, and keep your eyes on mine."

Lisa sat down and stared at him.

"Now, smile ever so slightly with one corner of your mouth."

She lifted one side of her mouth in a silly, lopsided grin. The painter threw down his brush and waved his arms in the air.

"No, that goofy grin won't do. You have to look alive and mysterious at the same time. You must smile with your eyes. You must sparkle with life."

Lisa just sat in her chair with the goofy look still on her face.

"Lucy, do you have any ideas about how to achieve the right smile?" Leonardo asked.

Cupping her hands around Leonardo's ear, Lucy whispered, "I think I know how to fix it. She really loves her husband, right?"

"Right," Leonardo said.

"Okay then, if he suddenly appears, the sight of him will fill her eyes with love, and they will sparkle."

Leonardo nodded. "Yes, yes, I think that will do it!"

He asked one of his assistants to bring Giacondo in through the back door so Lisa would not see him until the last minute. Five minutes later, Giacondo tiptoed into the studio. At the sight of her husband, Lisa seemed to light up from inside, thinking her own secret thoughts. Her eyes sparkled with life and amusement.

"You're a genius, Lucy. Thank you," said the artist.

Lucy joined Wilbur in the corner of the room. Leonardo sat at his easel painting Lisa's now radiant expression. Giacondo stood behind her. The candlelight cast long shadows on the walls of the studio. Leonardo's flying machines swung from threads like prehistoric pterodactyls. Their voices grew muffled. A window seemed to open, and the artist, the girl, and her husband transformed into frozen images beyond it.

"Look at them, Wilbur," said Lucy. "They've turned into a painting behind a window. How did that happen?"

"The most important invention of Renaissance art," Wilbur said, "was creating the impression of looking through a window at a real scene. Come on, I have a surprise for you back in Florence."

Wilbur's green glow was fading to grey and he was beginning to limp. Her heart ached when she thought he might be in pain. *Please, let him be okay,* she prayed.

Chapter 10

The Man Who Loved Hard Boiled Eggs

Wilbur and Lucy flew from Vinci to Florence in two earth minutes. They passed through yet another of the plasma-like veils that separated time.

"It has been fifteen years since you helped Leonardo with Lisa's smile and art is very different now," said Wilbur.

"Wait a minute," said Lucy. "I want to know if Lisa liked the portrait."

"That's an interesting story," said Wilbur, as he flew in a circle around Lucy. "Leonardo never gave Lisa her portrait. He was such a perfectionist that he would not give it to her until he thought it was finished. But, then he decided to move to France and he took the painting with him. He died before he had a chance to give it to her so it has stayed in France ever since. Lisa must have had a fit."

"So she never even saw it?"

"No, she didn't," said Wilbur. "And I don't know if she ever found another artist to paint her portrait."

They landed behind an abandoned church near the center of Florence. Wilbur led Lucy to a modest white house on a quiet street.

"Young artists of this era are not interested in creating depth and making a painting look like a window leading to another world as Leonardo had been. They paint cold, glittering portraits of what a person looks like, but not who he is."

"You mean they forgot all about Leonardo?"

"No, Leonardo would always influence art, but you will see a different style when you meet the artist who lives here."

Lucy looked at her list. "Jacopo Pontormo, right?"

"Right," he said, knocking on the door. "He's a real character."

There was no answer so they pushed the door open and walked into an empty room with a high ceiling.

"Prepare yourself," said Wilbur, "Jacopo is a great artist, but he is also an oddball."

"What do you mean?" Lucy asked.

"For one thing, he lives in his attic and won't come down. And, he doesn't like most people so usually he doesn't open the trap door in the ceiling and throw down his rope ladder."

Lucy looked up at the trap door. "What else makes him odd?"

"Actually, I feel sorry for him," said Wilbur. "He's afraid of most people and he doesn't eat anything except hard boiled eggs. Call him; he might let us up"

"Mr. Jacopo, please open your trap door and let us up," called Lucy.

Wilbur and Lucy stood with their necks bent back waiting for an answer.

Suddenly, Jacopo burst through the trap door and hung upside with a hardboiled egg in his mouth. Lucy had to clap a hand over her mouth to keep from giggling.

"Hi, I'm Lucy and this is Wilbur. I've heard so many great things about your paintings that I had to visit you. Can we please come up?"

Jacopo gulped down the egg and said, "Since, you put it like that, okay. We can talk and have a picnic, and I might show you my new painting."

An old rope ladder tumbled down from the trap door.

"Careful, I made the ladder extra wobbly. If I change my mind about letting someone up, I can shake him off."

Wilbur climbed onto Lucy's back and put his legs around her neck, piggy back style. She held the rungs tightly and climbed up the swaying ladder to Jacopo's studio.

Sunlight poured through six windows. *What a perfect place for an artist to work*, Lucy thought. This was the studio that she had imagined when she stood on the lawn and made her wish. Canvasses leaned against the walls, sketchpads and paper littered the floor, bottles of turpentine, oil, simple furniture, and a mattress lay against a wall.

Wilbur found a comfortable chair near one of the windows, fastened his spectacles behind his pointy ears, and picked up a book entitled, *Only You Can Save the Perpendiculars from the Nidwaggles*.

Jacopo and Lucy sat on two low stools facing one another. He clasped his paint-stained hands together and leaned forward toward Lucy. His long, slender fingers reminded her of a pianist's hands. Once, Lucy and her mother heard a great pianist play a

Beethoven piano sonata. He had beautiful long fingers too. Musicians had to be precise, playing all the notes at just the right speed. Maybe, Jacopo's paintings were precise too. Maybe he painted careful, sharp edges.

"Sorry about the clutter," he said, looking around the attic, "but I don't invite many people up here and I like to have all my things around me when I work."

"Me too," said Lucy. "I spread my stuff out all over the place wherever I go. I'm always leaving things behind."

"Want a snack?" Jacopo said, clapping his hands.

His smile was so excited and hopeful that Lucy could not refuse.

"I'd love a snack," she said.

"I have hard-boiled eggs and hard-boiled eggs and more hard-boiled eggs. I usually boil six or seven dozen at one time. I hope you like them."

"I love them," Lucy said.

"Great," he said, hopping into another room to fetch the snack. He returned with two bowls filled with hard boiled eggs and two glasses of something.

"Here we are," he said, placing the feast on a nearby table. "Those are your eggs and that is your mango juice." He rubbed his hands together in eager anticipation and said, "These are mine."

As they peeled the eggs, Jacopo and Lucy talked about themselves.

"What interests you most?" He asked her.

"I am interested in practically everything, but my favorite thing is crystals."

"Crystals! How perfectly divine!" Jacopo said. "Why do you like them?"

"I like them because they seem to like me. My grandmother gave me a collection of quartz crystals that sparkle in the sun on my bookshelf. They're the most beautiful colors you've ever seen. Each one I hold gives me a different feeling."

"What do you mean they seem to like you?" Jacopo asked.

"Well, when I hold the pink one, I feel calm and sleepy. When I hold the purple one, I feel like picking flowers. And when I hold the blue one it reminds me of floating in the ocean. They all do something nice."

He looked into her eyes as though he were reading her mind.

"Is there something else about crystals that you're not telling me?" Jacopo asked.

Lucy was amazed. "Yes, it happened this morning, at least I think it was this morning. I was wishing for something to help me. Suddenly, a small clear crystal that I had never seen before started blinking. It's smooth and flat and has beautiful gold slivers running through it. It warmed my hand and made me feel safe. I think it might be magic."

"Why did you need help?" Jacopo said.

It was hard for Lucy to talk about what had happened in class the day of her report.

"Something awful happened to me in school. In the middle of a report, I couldn't remember anything. I just stopped talking and got so scared that I fainted. Now I'm afraid it'll happen again and everyone will laugh at me."

Jacopo looked as if he were about to cry.

"Do you know how many people feel just as afraid as you do? I am just as scared as you are, not about speaking out loud in front of people. I'm afraid to show people my paintings because I think they will laugh at me."

"But painting something isn't like falling down in class," said Lucy.

"But it is. When an artist shows people his paintings, he is standing in front of thousands of people, showing them his whole heart and hoping that they will like him. I have exactly the same fears as you. If my painting is rejected, I feel stupid and humiliated. It's the loneliest feeling in the world."

Lucy had never thought about this, but it must be true. Even a genius has worries, especially one like Jacopo, who doesn't fit in. *No wonder he's afraid to leave this attic,* thought Lucy. *I'm going to cheer him up.*

"You have probably noticed that I'm not like a normal person," said Jacopo, peeling eggs and popping them into his mouth.

87

Lucy started to disagree with him to make him feel better, but he quickly said, "It's alright, I know I'm not like those people who can get up and get dressed and be happy all day. I also know that I am just as scared of people laughing at me as you are."

"But, if you were one of those normal people," said Lucy, "you would see the world in the boring, regular way everybody sees it and you wouldn't be able to paint like you do. I bet your paintings are as surprising as you are. It's good for your paintings that you're not a regular person."

He scooped up all the egg shells and tossed them out the window. Lucy was not about to toss garbage out the window; she would probably conk some poor fifteenth-century monkey on the head. She looked around the room for a plate or bowl.

"Not to worry, here take this," Jacopo said, offering her a bowl in the shape of a chicken.

I think we are kindred spirits, Lucy," said Jacopo. "I'm not afraid to show you one of my paintings."

Lucy rested her chin in her hands and watched the artist lift a six-foot painting from a pile of canvasses leaning against the wall. She had been expecting something different, but not in her wildest dreams had she imagined such a magical painting.

Lucy caught her breath. The painting was fantastic. Four very tall women, wearing bright pink, orange, and green dresses stood in a circle on the very edge of the canvas. In fact, they were giants, looming over Lucy as though standing on a stage right in front of her. They seemed so close to her that she felt they might topple off the stage and fall on her.

Unlike Leonardo's painting, there was no mist, there was no depth, and there was no attempt to show the personality of the women. When she looked at the Mona Lisa, Lucy could see Leonardo's delicate brushstrokes. Jacopo's brushstrokes were invisible. She had been right about his precision. The women's dresses fell in folds in sharp angles.

"Well?" Jacopo asked, raking his fingers through his hair, "What do you think?"

"I feel like the wind has been knocked out of me," said Lucy. "I've never seen anything like it. You see bigness and bright color in the world and that's different from any other artist."

"So you like it?"

"I love it. I'll never ever forget it. Everything is a surprise. The colors are more dazzling than my crystals. The women are giants with large, round, serious eyes, and they make me feel unbalanced because they could fall into the room any minute."

"Strange colors and tall people are my signature," Jacopo said, proudly. "But, now you can see why I'm afraid that people might laugh. My painting is just like me-unbalanced and a little crazy."

"But, it's the energy and craziness that makes it so brilliant," said Lucy. "When I look at it, I feel as if I know you."

Once again, Lucy saw that an artist's personality can be seen in his paintings.

"Thank you, Lucy," he said. "You've helped me a lot. Before I met you, I didn't know that there were other people who are just as scared and nervous as I am."

Wilbur took off his glasses and put the book back where he had found it. Their visit with Jacopo was over.

"Thanks for the snack, Jacopo," said Wilbur.

"But, you didn't have any eggs. Hey, you can talk."

"You're not shocked, are you?" Wilbur asked.

"I'm a nut. Nothing shocks me," said Jacopo.

Lucy and Wilbur climbed down the rope ladder.

"Bye," said Jacopo, "I'll miss you."

The trap door slammed shut, but beyond it, they heard the faint whistle of a happy tune. Lucy knew there was something very wrong with Wilbur. He had slept through the whole visit and his limp was worse. She felt his forehead with her hand. He was burning up with fever. There might be times when he would bounce back, but in her heart, she knew he was getting sicker and sicker. And, that thought made her even more determined to take care of him. The thought of losing him terrified her.

Chapter 11

Buried Alive

The bright green light that had glowed from within Wilbur's body flickered and changed color. As they made their way from Jacopo's house to the garden where they were supposed to fly to Rome to meet Michelangelo, Lucy checked the Navigator. She remembered how alive it had felt the first time she held it in Wilbur's house. Now, it felt as limp and sad as he looked.

She carried him as they walked across the Arno River up the hill to another splendid palace with magnificent gardens.

"I know you have decided to take care of me," said Wilbur. "I am feeling weak so you will have to do some of the work, but you must follow my directions exactly. Carry me down that path until I tell you to stop. I will show you how the Navigator works."

Lucy carried Wilbur down a shell-covered path lined with pink rhododendrons. They passed water streaming down narrow channels and marble sculptures of Greek gods and goddesses. She loved being so close to him. Tears filled her eyes, as she realized that he was in pain. His head lay trembling on her chest and, every so often, a silky ear twitched against her cheek.

"Don't cry, Lucy. No one knows what will happen. Let's stop here. It looks like a good place to take off for Rome. Let's talk about the Navigator for a minute."

Lucy helped Wilbur onto a stone bench beside a path of crushed shells. The Navigator looked as dull and as sick as Wilbur. She stroked his back while they looked through the crystal dome. A trail of tiny diamonds on a map of Italy indicated their flight plan from Florence to Rome, where they would meet Michelangelo.

"The pointy diamonds mark our course back and forth through time to our destinations. The Dispatcher communicates these coordinates to the Navigator so that it can guide us to the right place. Now they are marking the way to Rome. Do you understand?"

Lucy nodded.

Wilbur said, "As you can see, I am very sick. That means there is also something wrong with the Navigator. If the trail drifts or moves, it means the Navigator is not steering us on the right course. We might be in danger."

"I understand," she said.

Tall pine trees that looked like umbrellas made circles of shade on the ground. She lowered him gently onto a bed of slippery pine needles.

Wilbur wriggled out of Lucy's arms and pulled a satin collar embroidered with pearls from one of his fur pockets.

"I have to look my best. The Romans take fashion very seriously."

Lucy fastened the collar around Wilbur's shrinking neck.

"Now, it's time to meet the great and explosive Michelangelo."

"What do you mean explosive?" Lucy asked.

"He has a terrible temper."

With Wilbur curled in her arms, they rose above the rooftops of Florence. Each time Lucy's feet left the ground, her insides giggled. It was like riding a Ferris wheel, only a million times better.

The wind blew Wilbur's pointy ears flat against his head. His mouth hung open in exhaustion. A few minutes into their flight, Wilbur put a paw over Lucy's eyes.

"Don't look down!" He ordered.

Lucy pushed his paw aside and looked down. If they had been on the right course they would have seen the Coliseum in Rome. Unfortunately, what they saw were miles and miles of desert below.

"What's happening?" She said, grabbing the Navigator from her pocket. The diamond trails were going crazy, crisscrossing and leading nowhere. Lucy held Wilbur tighter.

"It's either broken or possessed by an evil force. There are lots of books on earth about this. It's going to dump us in the desert to die of thirst," she said.

Wilbur reached for her shoulder and said, "Calm down. There could be a perfectly logical explanation for the sand. Maybe a sand storm covered all of Rome for a few minutes in the sixteenth century."

"Please don't be silly," said Lucy. "This is serious."

She was right. It was very serious because the light that glowed from Wilbur and the Navigator was now a ferocious shade of turquoise.

Suddenly, white light flashed in their eyes and the next second they lay in pitch darkness on a cold, stone floor. Lucy's arms were empty. Panicky, she wondered if she had dropped Wilbur in the sand.

Her voice echoed through the darkness, as she called, "Wilbur, are you here? Are you alright?"

His faint voice answered her from far away. Wilbur wheezed, "Yes, Lucy, I am still with you."

She crawled across the sandy floor in the direction of his voice.

"What is this awful place?" She said.

"I'm not sure," said Wilbur, "But I don't like it. My claustrophobia is acting up."

Lucy screamed when something slithered over her leg.

"Oh, please help me! I'm so scared of snakes."

As she scurried away, her hand bumped into something small and metal with a handle and spout.

"I think I've found a lamp," she shouted.

"Keep following my voice," he said.

She crawled toward his voice until she felt a bushy tail, then his back, and then her hands found his face. She remembered that he had told her that magic was too big for small things.

"Listen, Wilbur, I don't care how big magic is, it's not too big to give us some light, so would you please light this lamp?" She said, pushing it into his paws.

"Humph," he said.

The lamp flamed and lit up a large stone chamber with paintings on all the walls. In the dim light of the lamp, Lucy could see gold chairs, beds, and small statues glinting against a wall. She took off her sweater and wrapped it around Wilbur's shivering little body. They sat huddled together on a raised slab of stone. He was a pitiful figure, small and forlorn, sitting hunched over with his chin in his paws. A glaring, turquoise light glowed from his body and made his fur stand out in angry spikes. Every so often, a flash of turquoise light shot out of his blue eye. He had lost more of his solid bulk. Little by little, he was wasting away. Lucy felt as though her heart was breaking.

"Why are you so sick?" Lucy asked, hugging him closer and holding his paw.

His answer was a faint whisper.

"When I heard your wish and planned the trip, I thought that if my wavelengths were connected to the Navigator's, then if anything happened to it, the Dispatcher could guide me."

"But would that make you sick too?" Lucy asked.

"I'm sick because viruses infect wavelengths on the same frequency, which is how the Navigator infected me. The heart of a Wise One is his mind and his wavelengths are like the arteries in your body, only they pump energy rather than blood."

"Are you going to die?" Lucy asked, in a panicky voice.

"I will die if we don't fix the Navigator."

"But, why don't you use magic to fix it?" Lucy asked. "Saving your life is certainly big enough for magic."

For the first time, the corners of Wilbur's mouth hung down in misery.

In a soft voice, he said, "My magic is more limited than you think. When I am guiding a child toward self-realization, I can fly, light lamps, and do a bunch of things by blinking. I wanted to help you very much, but I have never traveled back in earth time. The virus that is killing the Navigator is an earth compound, of which I have no knowledge. As an earth being, you are more likely to know what to do than I am."

The speech had used up all his strength. He lay down on the slab with a thud.

Lucy was frantic. "But I don't know anything about compounds! I'm getting C's in science class."

Then she had an idea.

"We'll just go home after I find a way out of here. You can go back to your planet and get well and I'll see my parents. My report doesn't matter."

"I'm afraid that's impossible," said Wilbur. "The program I wrote for the Dispatcher and the Navigator is unchangeable so we cannot go home until we have completed the journey I planned."

His eyelids were heavy. "I am so tired, Lucy. I am going to take a little nap."

"No, wait," screamed Lucy. "You have to tell me what to do. I'm afraid."

The chamber was absolutely silent except for Wilbur's soft snoring. Lucy took the Navigator out of her pocket. Its rim was rusted and its dome was smeared with moisture blotting out the constellations and maps. A dull light blinked once and then it went dark.

It's fallen into a coma, she thought, praying that Wilbur was still conscious. Shaking him gently, he groaned and wheezed something about Red Dwarves.

She tried whacking the Navigator on the stone floor, shaking it, she even tried scolding it. "Listen, you rickety, metal hockey puck thing, start working, or you'll never see your friend, the Dispatcher, again."

A dribble of turquoise liquid leaked from one of the switches. Lucy was cold and scared inside the massive chamber. For the first time, she noticed a large, stone coffin, its lid pushed to one side, in the middle of the chamber. Her heart raced as she put it all together: the painted stone walls, the coffin, the pointed ceiling. She and Wilbur were trapped inside an Egyptian pyramid and it was only a matter of hours before they suffocated. She had to investigate the tomb, starting with the coffin.

Chapter 12

The Steady Gaze of Tawosret

As Lucy leaned over the coffin, her hair spilled onto the decaying skeleton of an Egyptian mummy, still wrapped in its tattered rags. She cried out, pushed herself away, and tripped over a gold cat sculpture with emerald green eyes. A chill ran down her spine. Maybe it was finding the cat, or maybe it was her imagination, but for the first time, Lucy knew that she and Wilbur were not alone.

A deafening noise, like blocks of stone grinding together, came from the far corner of the chamber. Her heart pounded hard in her chest, as she tip toed toward the terrible noise. All at once, a giant stood in front of her. He stood absolutely still inside a shallow niche cut in the wall. His face was solemn; his black eyes glittered as they stared at the wall over Lucy's head. The man wore a gold and blue striped crown and a folded skirt. His naked arms and clenched fists were stiff and rigid at either side of his body. One leg was extended in front of the other in an uncomfortable pose. A picture of Sam's book came to mind. *This isn't a live man,* she thought, excitedly. *It's Tawosret, the pharaoh from Sam's book!*

The awful screeching noise started up again and, to her horror, the colossal statue stepped out of the niche and moved steadily toward Lucy. She gasped and stumbled backwards, falling onto the sandy floor. Two beams of light flashed from its black eyes.

It's going to steamroll over me, she thought.

"Help me, Sam," she whispered.

The last thing she expected to hear was Sam's calm, monotone voice, but she did hear it, echoing inside the tomb.

"Think and remember," he said.

How in the world had Sam heard her call for help?

Then she remembered their conversation about his steady gaze. *Maybe, Tawosret's spirit is inside the statue and can see me. If he's lonely, maybe he'll gaze steadily at me and help me,* she thought.

The statue had stopped just short of Lucy's feet. She gathered all her courage and said, "If you are inside there, your highness, could you help me and my friend escape? We're both going to suffocate soon so the quicker the better."

The statue's crystal eyes slid toward one of the painted walls. *A clue,* she thought, running to the wall painting. In the flickering lamplight, Lucy saw a painting of the pharaoh standing on a magic boat, looking up at a cluster of stars. Everything her mother had told her about the ancient pharaohs flying to the stars in a magic boat was true. Her heart beat with excitement as she remembered exactly how they had done it. Sam had told her that there were tunnels leading from the tomb to the constellation Orion's Belt. She had to find the tunnels fast.

It might have been a trick of the light, but, when Lucy turned around to thank Tawosret, it seemed the corners of his mouth lifted into the slightest of smiles.

"Thank you, Tawosret," she said. "You can go back to steadily gazing now."

Wilbur was still asleep on the stone slab when she made her way back to him.

She bent close to his ear, and said softly, "Wilbur, wake up. There's a secret passageway out of here somewhere. I'm going to find it so we won't die."

His eyes fluttered, as he lifted his heavy head and murmured, "Don't bother me. I'm dancing a jig with my friend, MacSpurtle. He's a Scottish muskrat who cooks delicious brootles."

He's delusional, thought Lucy. *Time's running out.*

That is when the lamp flickered out. She would have to find the opening to the tunnel in the dark. Groping her way across the chamber, she laid her palms flat on the wall and moved her arms in circles until one of her hands dropped into a square opening

"Wilbur, wake up," she called, but he did not answer her. She crawled back to him, gave him a gentle shake and said, "Wilbur, it's me, wake up."

103

His voice was slurry when he spoke. "Is it time for the brootle soup yet?"

"You're hallucinating," said Lucy. "You have to stop thinking about jigs and brootles and Scottish muskrats, and listen to me."

He sat halfway up, rubbing his eyes. As if seeing her for the first time, he smiled dopily at her and said, "Lucy, where have you been? For that matter, where are we?"

"That moron Navigator dropped us into an ancient Egyptian pharaoh's tomb inside a pyramid. Luckily, the pharaoh's spirit is still down here inside a statue, and he told me how to escape."

"Huh?" Wilbur said, confused at first, then his eyes flew open, and he shouted, "What? There is a talking statue nearby?"

"No," said Lucy, "He didn't talk at all; he signaled with his eyes, that's all. You didn't miss much. But, I know how we can escape before we suffocate. How do you feel?"

"I feel a little better."

Lucy helped him walk over to the wall with the opening to the tunnel.

"You're not going to like it, but we have to crawl through a tunnel in order to get out of here. Just watch out for scorpions and snakes that could eat you up in one bite."

"What a horrid thought!" Wilbur said.

Lucy pushed his behind through the opening before hoisting herself inside. Lying on her stomach, dragging her velvet dress with the comatose Navigator in her pocket through centuries of dust, she inched forward on her elbows.

"I'm going to look awful when we get out of here," she said. "My hair is a tangled mess and this stupid dress is filthy."

Wilbur grumbled, as he stumbled up the narrow passageway. "I don't like this place one little bit. It's the absolute worst thing for a claustrophobic. Look at me, I'm shuddering."

Lucy smiled. *At least he hasn't lost his sense of humor.*

At first, there was only a pinprick of light far off in the distance. Then the light grew as bright and as luminous as a pearl in the dark sky.

"It's the moon, Wilbur!" Lucy said.

At last, they were able to climb out of the tunnel onto one of the huge blocks of stone on the exterior of the pyramid. The awful turquoise light that had infected Wilbur turned soft green. Lucy lifted the Navigator out of her pocket and, holding it in the palm of her hand, she said to it, "There, don't you feel better out here? Moonlight and starlight will help you." She held it high in the air, as close to the stars as possible. Soon, a pale green light glowed from within it. Lucy jumped into the starry sky with Wilbur in her arms and the Navigator clutched in her hand. They circled the desert and then flew northwest toward Rome and Michelangelo.

Chapter 13

Grumpy Michelangelo

"Look, Wilbur," Lucy shouted, jolting him awake. "There's the Coliseum. We're in Rome and there's no sand!"

Mist hung like clouds above the streets of Rome. As they walked along the Tiber River, Lucy heard the sounds of sixteenth-century life on the street - the clip clop of horses, muffled laughter, the melodic strumming of a mandolin. Still wrapped in her sweater, Wilbur was a small, limping form, barely visible through the drizzle. He stopped in front of a dilapidated house with a brass plaque on the front door engraved with 'Buonarotti.'

"Who's Buonarotti?" Lucy asked.

"Michelangelo's last name is Buonarotti. We can drop the pet routine with him too. He believes statues live inside blocks of marble so a talking dog will seem perfectly normal."

"What's he like?" Lucy said.

Wilbur said, "From what I have heard, he complains quite a bit, especially about his low salary and his house. The pope is paying him to paint the Sistine ceiling and, according to Michelangelo, he pays him only a few ducats every now and then."

"How much is he getting to paint the entire ceiling?" Lucy asked.

"Well, let's see," said Wilbur, "A ducat is about five dollars, so I guess he will be getting about two hundred earth dollars."

"That's crazy!" Lucy said. "I can't believe it. Is there anything else I should know about him?"

"He has a terrible temper," said Wilbur. "One time, he got into a fight with another artist who broke his nose."

"He sounds kind of scary," said Lucy.

"The thing about Michelangelo is that he feels unloved. So just be nice to him. Let him talk about himself. He is not like Leonardo, who knows that everything he does is wonderful. Michelangelo worries about everything, but mostly, he is worried that this ceiling painting isn't good."

"But, how could he think that?" Lucy said. "The Sistine ceiling is the most beautiful art in the world."

"Other people see that," said Wilbur, "But, he doesn't see himself as a great artist."

"Okay, then, I'll be very nice to him," said Lucy.

Wilbur pointed to an upstairs window and said, "Shout something at that window up there. Let's try to get him to let us in. He's probably hammering on a block of marble so he wouldn't hear the knocker."

"What should I say?" Lucy asked.

"Um," said Wilbur, "Tell him he's a genius."

Lucy nodded and shouted, "Mr. Buonarotti, I am Lucy, a lowly, regular person with hardly any ideas, and I would be honored if I could come up and listen to your wonderful ideas."

The wooden shutters of a second story window bashed open and a candle floated into the darkness over their heads.

A gruff voice said, "I'm especially grouchy tonight, but since you asked so nicely, come in. The door is open. Wait, is that a dog? I'm allergic to dog fur."

"It's okay," said Lucy. "You won't be allergic to Wilbur. He's not a typical dog. He's very clean, his fur never comes out, and he talks."

Wilbur held up a paw and said, "Greetings, oh most excellent one. Nasty weather we're having."

"It's even worse in here," said the voice. "Come on in and we'll talk about all my problems."

Water dripped into buckets inside the cramped hallway. Michelangelo stood at the top of a rickety flight of stairs. Lucy's first reaction was shock because the great artist was neither handsome like Leonardo or Botticelli, nor was he dopey and fun like Jacopo. Michelangelo was a big man with a crooked nose and a mop of messy, dark hair that stuck to his forehead. Sweat-smeared marble dust and charcoal covered his face and arms. This burly, frowning man, wearing a leather tunic and lace up sandals, was the opposite of Leonardo in his velvet capes and hats with feathers. As she walked past him at the top of the stairs, Lucy saw intensity of feeling and sadness in his eyes.

The artist led them into a room crowded with statues that looked like ghosts in the dim candlelight. Lucy accidentally stepped on Wilbur's bushy tail.

"Ow," he yelped.

"I'm sorry," said Lucy.

Wilbur put his paw in her hand so that she would not feel badly.

Water dripped through the ceiling onto Michelangelo's hair and face. He looked like he was going to explode with anger.

"I'm going to get the plague living in this wet, broken down hut," he shouted. "I have to sleep on a bed of wet straw. I have no money for snacks and all I ever eat is radish soup."

"Why?" Lucy asked.

"Why?" He repeated. "I'll tell you why. I was dragged away from my nice house in Florence to this awful hut to paint a ceiling. And, I never get paid," he said, pacing around the room, rubbing his big hands together. "In fact, I have to beg my father and brother for money."

He blinked as though something was in his eyes. Then, he closed them, saying, "Wait just a minute. I have paint in my eyes."

He poured a bucket of water over his head and said, "Ahh, that's better."

"Why do you have paint in your eyes?" Lucy asked.

"Because I stand on a wooden scaffold, which is a platform so I can reach the ceiling and the paint splatters in my eyes. My neck and shoulders are sore and I'm growing a hump on my back."

"See?" He turned around so Lucy could see his hump.

She could not see a hump. Michelangelo kept on talking.

"I had to fire all my assistants because they sloshed paint all over the place. So now I have to mix the paints, smooth the plaster, and paint all by myself, and…"

"Just a minute," said Lucy, "I thought you painted the ceiling lying down on a platform."

"What nincompoop told you that? Look at this."

He whipped out a cartoon that showed a man standing with his head thrown back, painting with one raised arm. Five hairs sprouted out of the top of his head like a rooster crown.

"Is this you?" Lucy asked, smiling.

"Yes, and it's not funny," he said, pointing to a verse written beside the picture. "I wrote a poem about paint splattering in my eyes and the hump that's growing on my back."

Lucy held the paper with the cartoon, thinking that someday, if it survives, this drawing would be an important document. It proved that Michelangelo stood while he painted the ceiling and it showed how insecure he felt.

Now, he was ranting about the light. Careening around the room, bumping into one statue then another, he said, "How am I supposed to sculpt in the dark?"

He's going to have a heart attack if he doesn't calm down, thought Lucy.

Lurching away from a tall statue, he stubbed his toe and howled in pain.

"Ow! You stupid, stupid rotten sculpture! I'll show you," he shouted at the top of his lungs.

110

Lucy could not believe her eyes when he grabbed a big hammer and smashed an arm off the sculpture.

"How could you do that? It's ruined," she said.

"It looks better this way," grumbled Michelangelo.

He looked apologetically at her and said, "I'm sorry for shouting. I am very unhappy here. I don't like to paint. Painters like that Leonardo da Vinci get on my nerves. The only thing I'm good at is sculpting. Maybe you've heard of my sculpture of David. It's won lots of prizes."

Lucy had seen the David in the main square in Florence.

"Yes, I saw it and I think it's awesome," she said.

He smiled and said, "Yes I guess it does inspire awe in everyone. So anyway, ever since I got here, I've been in a horrible mood because it's too dark to sculpt when I get home at night."

"I can understand how awful it must be," said Lucy.

She did understand him. He was a sad genius, who loved to sculpt so much that even though he was tired when he got home, he still wanted to work.

Michelangelo raked his dirty fingers through his hair. His eyes were filled with despair.

Lucy said, "Maybe we can think up a way to make it light enough for you to see what you're doing."

"Yes, please help me. Here's a stool, sit down," he said.

Lucy sat down and thought- *Miners! Miners wear hats with strong flashlights on their heads. Michelangelo can make himself a miner's hat using a candle.*

111

"I have an idea," she said.

"What is it?" He said, looking desperately at her.

"Make yourself a hat from stiff paper and glue a candle to the visor. That way, the candle will give you enough light to see what you are sculpting."

His eyes lit up. "Could that work? Yes, I think it will help me see the details of my carving. Oh, Lucy, thank you so much. Would you like to see why it's important for me to see details when I sculpt?"

She nodded.

He walked her to one of the sculptures and said, "Touch the marble here."

He put Lucy's fingers on the rough surface of an unfinished sculpture. She felt a network of fine lines crisscrossing the surface like a rough veil.

"I invented a new kind of chisel that lets me carve in this cross hatching pattern. Little by little, my sculpture comes to life. Thanks to you, now I will be much happier. I might even paint a good ceiling."

That's an understatement, thought Lucy.

"I would love to see your painting. Could we go there now?"

"I'll be in your debt forever, Lucy," said Michelangelo. "I'll take you to see it."

Michelangelo, Lucy, and Wilbur walked across the Tiber River to the grounds of the Vatican, where the Sistine Chapel had been built. They followed him through dark corridors lit by fiery sticks attached to the walls. Michelangelo stopped in front of a pair of large wooden doors with iron rings for handles.

"Here we are," he said, pulling open the door.

Nothing could have prepared Lucy for the feeling of being inside that chapel. The room was smaller than she had expected. It was long and thin, with a curved ceiling. At one end, wooden scaffolding reached up to the part of the ceiling that Michelangelo was painting. A bridge attached to a track ran across the width of the room. The track allowed the bridge to slide forward so that Michelangelo could move down the length of the ceiling as he finished each part.

"How are we going to get up there?" Lucy asked. She did not bother to ask Wilbur why they could not simply fly up.

Michelangelo led them to a makeshift elevator attached to the scaffolding and said, "We ride up."

They stood on the wooden platform and the artist began to hoist them up sixty feet in the air by pulling on a rope. The elevator stopped with a jolt when it came level with the scaffold floor. Michelangelo knotted the rope around a cleat and led them onto the bridge.

Lucy and Wilbur bent their heads all the way back, stunned by the wonder that spread across the curved ceiling above them. All of the figures appeared to be floating against the sky, but the spectacular figure of God that loomed over them seemed capable of tearing through the plaster ceiling itself. Lucy shrank beneath the ferocious, bearded God whizzing through the sky with his arms spread apart, one arm pointing behind at the huge newly-created moon and the other thrust forward in the direction of the orange sun.

Lucy reached up and ran her fingers over the painted surface.

"All of the people on the ceiling look like huge sculptures," she said. "Your painting even looks sort of like a carving. These crisscross lines remind me of your statues."

"You are very observant, Lucy," said Michelangelo. "As I told you, I am a sculptor first so I paint the way I sculpt, creating roundness and dimension using a cross hatched brushstroke."

"Why did you make these people flying in front of the sky?" She asked.

"I painted the sky on the ceiling because it creates the impression the roof is really open to the sky and that makes the room look bigger and airier."

Wilbur pushed against Lucy's leg.

"I am sorry, Michelangelo," said Lucy. "We have to go now. Thank you for bringing us here and for teaching me so much."

Michelangelo looked down at her and said, "My dear Lucy, thank you. Because of you, I will be able to sculpt all night. Goodbye."

As they walked out of the chapel, Wilbur said, "Off we go, Lucy. Hopefully, the Navigator will behave. With luck, it will lead us to France where we will meet your favorite artist. Are you ready?"

Chapter 14

Hannibal and His Darling Elephants

Lucy held Wilbur like a baby, flying northwest over swamps and lovely grassy hills with Greek temples and Roman villas, then they were over sunflower fields, and finally they reached the snow-capped mountains of the Alps. Snow dusted Wilbur's face and his furry paws and Lucy's hair and eyelashes. She thought she had never seen anything as beautiful as the sights below them-moonlit mountains, sparkling rivers, and glassy lakes.

Bam! An ominous ray of violet light shot out of the pocket of Lucy's red dress. The virus had taken hold of the Navigator and Wilbur again. This time they were a virulent purple, like rotten grape juice.

"Oh no, there's no green in you at all, Wilbur," cried Lucy. "You're this gross shade of purple, like cough medicine. What hap...?"

She never got a chance to finish her sentence. One minute they were having a perfectly wonderful time flying over mountains and the next moment they lay face down in the snow on a jagged peak in the Alps. Miniature purple icicles hung from Wilbur's fur, nose, and even his eyelashes.

"Where are we?" She asked.

"I fear our small, round friend with the switches has flung us into the Alps," he said, pointing to where the Navigator lay pulsing in her pocket.

She inched forward on her elbows and whispered, "I don't want it to hear us in case it's turned into some sort of evil killing machine. Should we act normal?"

"Yes," said Wilbur. "Act as if is perfectly normal to be thrown into a snow drift in the Alps. It shouldn't know that we know that it's sick again, or it might just as well kill us now. Does that make sense?"

"Not really," said Lucy. "If it is sick and evil, it will kill us anyway."

Suddenly, the ground trembled with the pounding of gigantic footsteps.

"What was *that?*" Lucy whispered.

On the horizon, a giant, followed by a herd of elephants, thundered toward them.

"Actung! Meine Farfulfetcher Helphantastiker!" He shouted, his voice echoing throughout the walls of the icy chasm below.

This whole turn of events-the jagged peaks, the ice and snow, a possibly sadistic Navigator, and now a huge, bellowing man- could only mean big trouble.

Pointing to the man surrounded by a herd of elephants, Lucy said, "Tell me that weight lifter over there is a mirage."

"He's real alright," said Wilbur. "We are about to meet General Hannibal crossing the Alps with his sixty seven war elephants."

"You mean that scary man wearing animal skins and a bear's head is the actual Hannibal, the guy from the Punic Wars? I gave a report about him. It was awful. My mind went blank and I fainted."

"What a coincidence," said Wilbur, standing up and brushing off the snow. "Listen, he's singing to his elephants."

"What is he singing?"

Wilbur put a paw to one ear, and said, 'He's singing 'Careful, my darling elephants, it is slippery here and I would be very sad if one of you turned an ankle.'"

Lucy felt like giggling, but the situation was too frightening. After all, they were on a freezing mountain peak with a possessed Navigator and a maniac with a herd of elephants.

"We don't have time to listen to that caveman sing!" Lucy said, reaching into her pocket. "We have to fix this widget thing before it spins completely out of control."

But Wilbur had not heard her. He had wandered over to the edge of the cliff, popping Wilwahren raisins into his mouth while studying the icy chasm below.

Lucy grabbed him by the tail.

"Wilbur, you'll fall off the edge and be killed because you probably think magic is too big for a little thing like saving your life."

"Goodness me!" Wilbur said, choking on one of the alien raisins.

He looked bewildered and weary. His smiling mouth hung open and his eyes bulged. Lucy's heart pinched when she saw how ill he was. His body glowed purple through his fur, now zinging straight out like electrocuted wires.

Lucy said, "We have to get you off this freezing mountain."

Hannibal was almost upon them.

"That man looks like he kills live things with his bare hands. I bet he eats raw meat," said Lucy, holding Wilbur tightly.

A shadow loomed over them. Hannibal plucked Wilbur out of Lucy's arms and swung him off the ground.

"*Fortjshunge meine schonefeide!*" He bellowed.

"What did he say?" Lucy asked.

Wilbur choked.

"He said, 'Oh my word, what a beautiful little bundle.'"

"He really said that?" Lucy asked, clapping her hand over her mouth.

She held the Navigator in her palm. It looked pathetically sick, bouncing in her hand as if it had hiccoughs. Jagged beams of purple light shot out from its switches. She gave it a gentle shake, but it only hiccoughed again. She bashed it lightly against a chunk of ice. The hiccoughs stopped and the Navigator beamed a purplish brown light.

"Don't worry, little Wilbur," she whispered. "I think I might have fixed it enough to get us back on track."

The Navigator clicked and looked better.

"Huh?" Wilbur said, stunned and confused.

Hannibal put Wilbur down and reached for Lucy.

"Don't even think about it, Mr. Cave Man. You're not going to get me," Lucy yelled, as she backed off the edge of the mountain peak and plunged toward the frozen chasm.

"Help me, Wilbur, I'm going to die!" She screamed.

Chapter 15

What Do You See, Lucy

In a flash, the mountains and snow disappeared and Lucy and Wilbur were once again whizzing through the cool night sky with the Navigator safe in her pocket. By the time the light of dawn colored the horizon, the air was sweet and warm, and the sun was a disc burning away the blue sky around it. A vast cornfield lay below them.

"Now where are we," Lucy asked, looking down on the long rows of corn.

"We are in southern France in the year 1889, near the village of St, Remy," said Wilbur.

"Is this where we're going to meet Vincent van Gogh?" She asked.

"Yes, he is in the asylum here. Let's land and make our way through the cornfield."

They landed on one of the chalky paths that divided the rows of new corn. Dust billowed around them when their feet touched the ground. Wilbur snapped his toes and Lucy's red velvet gown became a brown dress with a white blouse and an apron. She also wore a starched white cap, a kerchief around her shoulders, and heavy brown shoes.

"I look like Cinderella in this hot, scratchy dress," said Lucy. "Can't you make a summer dress?"

"I am afraid that is the summer frock of choice this year," said Wilbur. "It's perfect. You'll blend in with every other milk maid in the area."

"Milk maid? Are there really such a thing as milkmaids?"

"Someone has to milk the cows," said Wilbur.

The heat was stifling. Sunlight streamed through the trellis of corn leaves overhead and reflected off the sandy path. Trails of dusty sweat trickled down Lucy's face, stinging her eyes. All around her was the squeak of crickets crashing into her burned legs. She slogged through the lumpy soil behind Wilbur, whose limp and wan color made him a pitiable little figure. Lucy yearned for the cool air of Florence at dawn when she and Wilbur stood on the Old Bridge and watched the water rush over the jetties.

Hot and miserable, she called, "How much longer, Wilbur? I think I have sunstroke."

"Nonsense," said Wilbur, sweeping a paw across the sky. "Concentrate on the here and now. Look at the baby corn and the blue sky. Even those entrancing little crickets tickling your legs are worth inspecting."

Whatever! Lucy thought.

"Let's talk about Vincent van Gogh," said Wilbur.

"What's an asylum?" Lucy asked.

"An asylum is a hospital where people go when they feel terribly sad."

"Poor Vincent, maybe I can cheer him up. I'll tell him how much everybody loves his paintings."

Wilbur stopped walking and faced her.

"Gracious me, you are having a hard time with the anomaly concept. You must not talk about anything that happened after 1889. Vincent will die never knowing how beloved he would become."

"That's just awful," said Lucy. "And it's not fair, when I could give him a reason to be happy. He probably wouldn't believe me, but at least I could try."

"You are right," said Wilbur. "He wouldn't believe you. His mind is in a dark place where he cannot hear praise. You might be able to see his sadness reflected in his paintings."

Lucy stopped walking in excitement.

"That's exactly what I'm supposed to be learning," she said. She had already gotten to know the other artists through their paintings.

She leaned down and stroked Wilbur's hot fur. He flinched under her touch.

"You're very sick, Wilbur. It even hurts when I pat you."

Pale grey light glowed from within him. The spring in his legs was gone. His shoulders slumped and his head looked heavy.

He ignored her and said, "Let's have a look at the Navigator."

The Navigator's switches and buttons hung like limp rubber around the rim.

Lucy drew in her breath and stamped her foot with frustration.

123

"Please listen to me. You're getting sicker by the minute and it looks like the Navigator is too."

"Yes, you're right," said Wilbur, wheezing. "We are succumbing to the virus faster than I predicted."

"Please don't die. I need you."

"Don't worry about that. We're here," he said.

Lucy and Wilbur emerged from the cornfield into a village of mossy-roofed houses and horse-drawn hay wagons. The hospital was a sprawling U-shaped building in front of them. To the left was an orchard of crabapple trees. Lucy felt relief when they passed through the front door into the cool front hall of the hospital. It took a few seconds for her eyes to adjust.

The walls of the asylum of St. Remy might have been white once, but now they were a dull grey. The rusted pipes that ran along the tops of the walls leaked and formed little puddles on the floor below. Women in long, white robes and huge hats with flying wings swept through the hallways.

Wilbur mumbled, *"Il est dans la chambre nombre* 345. *Bon, c'est juste."*

He was limping quite badly now so Lucy carried him upstairs. "What did that mean?" She asked.

"It was French for, "He is in room 345; good this way."

"How many languages can you speak?" Lucy asked.

He snuggled against her shoulder.

"On this planet, all of them; in this solar system, I am having difficulty with the language spoken on Saturn's sixty-seventh moon. Can you imagine inventing a language with no metaphors or past participles? Stop here."

They stopped in front of room number three hundred and forty-five. Wilbur lifted his paw about to knock when Lucy stopped him.

"Wilbur, let's think about this for a minute. He doesn't even know we're coming. Strangers might upset him."

"Nonsense," said Wilbur. "He is alone all day. He will love some company, especially a nice doggie like me."

"Okay, but I'm going to stand behind you."

Wilbur knocked and the door was opened by a thin young man with red hair. His eyes were blue and sad, but when he saw Lucy and Wilbur, his face lit up with joy.

"Good morning, what a nice surprise, come in," said the young man.

"Woof," Wilbur barked, hooking his back leg around Lucy's ankle and pulling her forward.

"Good morning," Lucy replied. "I'm Lucy Nightingale. I saw one of your paintings in Paris, and I loved it. Do you have any more that I could see?"

"My name is Vincent and yes, I will show you the painting I am working on now."

Vincent took Lucy's hands in both of his and led her into a cozy, pale blue room with a yellow bed tucked into the far corner. Lucy could not take her eyes off a painting of a pair of shoes. One of the shoes lay in a tattered mess with its laces undone upside down on top of the other shinier shoe. The painting spoke to Lucy of need and love. The tangled laces of the old shoe seemed to reach out like arms embracing its mate.

"That painting tells a story doesn't it?" she asked.

"What makes you say that, Lucy? It is just a still-life of two shoes, or do you see something more?"

Lucy worried that she might give the wrong answer. She wished that she had memorized something about Vincent's paintings. Her mouth felt dry and sticky.

Perceiving her fear, Vincent said, "There are no wrong answers, Lucy. There is only what your eyes and your soul tell you."

"That's what my teacher tells me," she said, "But I'm afraid my ideas won't be good enough."

"I know how frightening it is to express your thoughts and feelings," Vincent said, "But I continue to paint because I believe in my feelings. You will believe in yours if you keep trying."

Lucy was captivated by this sad man who spoke so passionately about feelings and ideas. She could see that he worried as much as she did about doing well.

"Okay, I'll keep trying," she said.

"Well then," Vincent said, "do me the favor of sharing your ideas about my painting."

"The shoes look alive," she said, pointing at one of them. "See, the upside down one looks like it needs the one underneath so much that it's almost smothering it. The laces are hugging it."

When she looked at Vincent, she was shocked to see tears dribbling down his cheeks.

"I'm sorry. Did I say something to make you sad?"

Vincent said, "You were able to see into my heart. The arrangement of the shoes symbolizes my love for my brother, Theo, who lives in Paris. That's a long way away, and I miss him very much."

Now she knew why the shoes looked so different. Vincent must see himself as the scuffed, old shoe and the clean, new shoe was meant to be his brother Theo. She checked on Wilbur. He was sleeping in a patch of sunlight.

Lucy wandered over to the nightstand beside Vincent's bed, piled with books by famous authors. On the bottom shelf was a book of Michelangelo's drawings. Maybe when Vincent looked at Michelangelo's drawing, he felt inspired by him and that was like a gift. Lucy held the memory of Michelangelo thanking her for his hat close to her heart like a secret gift.

She sat on the bed and said, "Why are you in this hospital?"

Vincent leaned back against a windowsill with his hands in his pockets. In front of him were his easel, his bottles of paint, and his brushes.

He said, "I am here because I have nightmares, and I feel sad and afraid all the time."

Lucy wished she could tell him how much everyone would love his paintings, that they would hang in museums all over the world, and that people would pay millions of dollars for them because they are so beautiful.

Suddenly, Vincent brightened, as if he had just made up his mind about something.

He said, "Do you like the night sky when there are stars and a bright new moon, Lucy?"

"I love the moon and stars. If I stare at the moon for a long time, I see magic things."

"Come over here then," he said.

Lucy joined him by the window. In front her, less than two inches away, was her favorite painting in the whole world, Vincent's *Starry Night*. Vincent pulled up a stool for her so they could look at the painting together.

"I had a feeling I was going to see a beautiful, stupendous painting when we came here and here it is," she said.

Vincent stood above her looking over her shoulder.

"What do you see, Lucy?" He asked.

She sat up straight and took a deep breath.

"I see the most wonderful painting in the world. I mean it's like whoa- a sky that looks like rolling ocean waves! It's so cool. Did you really see a sky like this?" She twisted around so she could see him.

Vincent's voice became dreamy. "I saw a frightening picture of nature in a dream. The stars were like comets and the moon looked like a flaming lamp. This sky is everything that scares me in the world. I am that dark village, helpless under the crushing weight of nature."

"Wow, that's really sad," she said.

Vincent nodded and said, "Keep going. Keep showing me my painting."

Lucy said, "When I look at the bright blue sky and the orange moon, I wish I had sunglasses. The colors frizzle each other."

Vincent laughed. "That is an excellent way to put it."

"But how do you do it?" She asked.

"Certain colors like orange and blue, or yellow and violet, have an intense effect on the eye when placed next to each other. What else do you see?" He asked.

Lucy followed the swift, curving brushstrokes with her finger.

"When I stand back everything moves, vibrates, or wriggles. The big dark tree on the left side looks like a scary monster."

Lucy squinted at the lower corner of the painting.

"There's a fingerprint beside your signature. What is it?" she asked.

"Since paintings express my emotions, I put the imprint of my thumb in all my painting."

"Cool," said Lucy, "I wish every artist painted the way you do."

"That would be very boring," said Vincent. "Every artist gives you his own glimpse of how he sees the world. To be great, you have to be brave enough to express what is in your heart."

Lucy wanted to tell Vincent about her worries. Maybe he could help her.

"Once, I forgot everything I had learned and I fainted in front of my whole class. Now I'm afraid that might happen every time I have to talk in front of people."

"When you feel that way," said Vincent, "throw yourself headlong into your work, and you will not be afraid."

He stood by the window sketching a baby's little cradle. It seemed to Lucy as if he had moved into a different world. The room shot away from her, carrying him away with it. Now, he was a small figure looking out the corner window of his room. She ran to Wilbur and held him. The room began to change. The blue paint melted and dribbled down the walls, revealing dirty, rusted plaster. Bars materialized over the windows. The yellow bed, table, chair, and pretty bottles of paint disappeared. It was no longer Vincent's warm, friendly room; it had become an ugly, dark cell with cracked walls, an iron bed, and a filthy mattress.

Wilbur stood up and held Lucy's hand.

"Is this the same room?" She asked.

"Yes," said Wilbur. "This is the way his hospital room really looked. Before, we were seeing what Vincent wanted us to see."

He patted her hand.

"It's so sad," said Lucy, "That this is the way he had to live-no books, no pretty yellow bed and blue walls, only a stinky bed, his paints in rusted tin cans, and that beautiful painting in a room like a prison cell."

Starry Night had followed Lucy when she ran to Wilbur. It stood front of them. Everything in the painting vibrated with life. As Lucy stared at the painting, it began to shudder and expand. Soon, it had engulfed the whole room, and the floor beneath their feet slipped away, propelling them into Vincent's seething blue sky.

Chapter 16

Marooned

Lucy caught Wilbur up in her arms just before the floor vanished beneath their feet and they fell forward into Vincent's dream night. She was shocked by the frailty of Wilbur's once-solid little body. A chilly wind, as swift and tumultuous as Vincent's sky, rolled over them and blew off tufts of Wilbur's fur. They landed on one of the hills in the background of the painting. Lucy laid him gently to the ground. She looked down at herself and saw that she had on her blue dress with the zippered pockets, her white sweater, and silver boots. Wilbur winced with pain and his teeth chattered, as she covered him with her sweater.

He looked into her eyes and wheezed, "I am so sorry I failed you, Lucy. We are marooned inside a painting where there will never be any daylight."

"No, we're not marooned," said Lucy. "I'm going to get us home. You close your eyes and rest. I'll be right back. I promise."

If she could not find a way to fix Navigator, Wilbur would die and she would never see her parents again.

She needed Sam. Hugging herself, she screamed as loudly as she could, "Help me, Sam! Please hear me."

His voice came to her, traveling across Vincent's waving sky and lamp-like moon. "You were right, Lucy, crystals do have a life force."

What does that mean? She thought. *And what does it have to do with fixing the Navigator?* She lifted the Navigator out of her pocket, holding it between her thumb and index finger. Moldy and limp, it sputtered and blinked, and then its light went out. She thought about how Sam had told her that quartz crystals were natural transmitters of radio frequencies. She had never asked Wilbur how the Navigator worked, maybe it did use some sort of crystal to power it. And maybe Sam meant that a crystal could be the secret of tuning to the Dispatcher's frequency.

"Where can I find a crystal here?" she called.

But Sam had gone, leaving Lucy alone on the black hill.

Maybe she could find one in the village below.

"I'll be right back, Wilbur," she said and she ran down the hillside, her silver boots sinking into the purple furrows of dirt. She turned back to check on Wilbur. Vincent's crashing sky rose up like a sea monster behind her. His thumbprint was a huge smear on the horizon. As bright as they were, the moon and stars did not light up the hills or the little town in the valley below. When Lucy reached the village, she found that it was only a painted curtain. There must be real village beyond the veil, but it frightened her. It was where Vincent's nightmares lived.

She took a running start and jumped through the veil. Now she was in a place so dark that only a sliver of Vincent's sky was visible. There were no cozy fireplaces or sleeping children tucked into bed. The houses were gaping, empty mouths without doors. She stood on a hard bumpy surface, slick with rain.

Groping through the soupy darkness, she called. "Hello? Is anyone here? Help me."

133

The thought of Wilbur alone on that cold hill made her insides hurt. He had been so kind to her and, for the first time she understood what he had meant when he said, 'We are taking the road to Lucy.' She also understood that he had risked his life for her.

Lucy felt her heart burst wide open. Gripping her sides, she bent over and howled. Her screams ripped through the air, and splashed on water. She straightened up and held her breath. If there was water close by, there might also be crystals because some crystal clusters grow in water. Spurred on by this thought, Lucy felt her way forward. Her hands hit a railing. Her footsteps were hollow under her feet. She was standing on a bridge. At the end of the railing, she slid down an embankment and waded in.

She stood up to her ankles in water. Squinting into the blackness she prayed that there were no clawing hands to pull her under as she waded in deeper. She reached into the water and felt around on the sandy bottom for a crystal. Her hand stirred up the sand. Dozens of crystals threw beams of colored light to the surface. Lucy grabbed the closest one, shoved it into the front pocket of her blue dress, and sped up the hill.

Wilbur lay motionless on the ground. Soft tufts of his beautiful fur lay around him like a funeral wreath. His head was thrown back exposing his fragile throat and the corners of his mouth drooped. His perky ears, so expressive in life, fell limp on either side of his head.

With shaking fingers, Lucy grabbed the Navigator and pried off the back. A frazzled, scorched crystal lay in a compartment inside. The virus had damaged it beyond repair. She removed the old crystal, pulled the one she had found in the water from her pocket, and inserted it into the compartment. Nothing happened. She waited. Still nothing happened. She ripped the crystal out of the Navigator and hurled it at Vincent's sky.

Inside the gaping hole where the Navigator's crystal had been, a rusty substance was spreading like fungus. Lucy scooped out as much as she could with her fingers. Then, she took off one of her socks and wiped it clean. What she saw reminded her of something familiar. A multitude of straight gold strips ran the length of the compartment. She was sure that these conductors were the secret to fixing the Navigator.

Her ears, fingers, and toes were freezing. Puffs of vapor issued from her mouth. She shivered in the cold wind that blew from the waves in Vincent's cobalt sky. It was so cold that icicles hung from Wilbur's fur. Her long hair hung in frozen locks around her shoulders. Her hands were so cold and numb that she stuffed them deep into her zippered pockets. Her fingers touched something small and glassy. She pulled it out and could hardly believe what she was seeing; it was the crystal that had shone so brightly that morning in her bedroom. Its gold needles glittered and vibrated with life in her palm. This was her last chance to save Wilbur.

Her fingers were shaking so violently from the cold that she had trouble inserting the crystal at the right angle. Its needles had to line up with the gold conductors of the Navigator. When she had it in place, she snapped on the back of the Navigator, and held it in her palm, watching and waiting. Minutes went by and nothing happened. Then Wilbur moaned. Lucy knelt over him with his paw in her hands. The Navigator flickered red. Wilbur blinked blue. Then, for one glorious moment, the Navigator and Wilbur emitted a blinding emerald light that turned Vincent's sky green.

Lucy's face was the first thing Wilbur saw when he opened his eyes. The ice on his eyes melted. She leaned over him and saw herself reflected in his blue eye. This time her reflection was not at all blurry, but it was as sharp as a cut crystal and her shadow was pointing in the right direction.

"You're going to be fine," she told Wilbur, kissing his ears. "I found the perfect crystal."

Wilbur smiled and whispered, "You see? There is magic in you."

The tufts of Wilbur's old fur blew away and vanished in Vincent's sky. New fur grew back thicker and shinier than ever. His barrel-shaped body assumed its balance and weight and his large ears flared like airplane wings. Best of all, his smile reached from ear to ear. Lucy had done it. She had saved his life and made it possible for them to go home. Wilbur reached a trembling leg around Lucy's neck and kissed her forehead.

"See, Wilbur, you didn't fail me," she told him. "You did exactly what you promised to do when we first met in the woods. I'm back on the Lucy road."

Wilbur told her, "That, and never forget that you saved my life."

Lucy said, "Do I get some sort of certificate proving it?"

He smiled. "I will make one and keep it for you on my mantel piece. Now are you convinced of your ability to form original ideas?"

"Yes, Wilbur, I am."

"Good," he said, "then let's go home."

When Wilbur dropped the glowing Navigator into one of his fur pockets, a warm feeling surged through Lucy. The crystal she had discovered would keep him safe forever.

Chapter 17

Good Bye

The Navigator purred in Wilbur's pocket as it received the coordinates from the Dispatcher, guiding them home. Lucy lay on Wilbur's back, looking up at the sky. The full moon and stars that twinkled around it were so different from Vincent's pulsing yellow moon and spinning stars. If she were to paint the sky at night, it would have a big, happy moon with twinkling stars around it.

Wilbur made a wide arc over his own house. He twisted a diamond switch that sent a command to the Dispatcher to initiate landing. Lucy landed on a bed of blue rose petals in the same closed garden where Wilbur had told her about Wilwahren and the Wise Ones. A cold stone dropped in her chest. Her time with Wilbur was almost over. She felt as though her heart were breaking. How could she say goodbye to him? Tears stung her eyes as she ran to find him. Racing past the potting shed and the blueberry bushes, past his wishing wells and birdbaths, she saw him under the blooming Chestnut tree in his rocking chair.

"Ahoy!" He called. "Don't you just love to fly at night? The best ideas pop into my head when I fly on a moonlit night. Sit with me for a bit"

Lucy stood over him pinching her bottom lip between her thumb and index fingers.

"What's the matter, Lucy? You smiled the whole way back."

Lucy knelt at his feet and took his paw in her hand.

"I'm afraid to leave you, Wilbur. Nothing will be the same."

"Fiddlesticks," he said. "You have an excellent sense of direction. You will never get lost again."

"What do you mean sense of direction?" Lucy asked.

"You found me, didn't you?" Wilbur said. "And, look how magnificently you solved the artist's problems."

"So what?" Lucy asked.

"So those great artists thought of you as a friend who helped them with your original ideas."

A table, set with a teapot and delicious food, appeared like magic between them.

"Oh goody!" Wilbur said, clapping his paws. "We have English muffins, strawberry jam, and my favorite- pineapple upside down cake."

I know exactly where I've heard that before, Lucy thought.

"Do you know Arabella Lang?" She asked.

Wilbur raised a paw like a policeman stopping traffic. "I cannot possibly discuss a former apprentice."

He handed Lucy a cup of tea and a piece of cake. "Yummy," he said, licking his chops.

While Wilbur was busy stuffing cake into his red mouth, Lucy wondered if he had learned anything from her.

"Wilbur," she asked timidly, "did you learn anything from me?"

"Oh my yes! I learned that one must risk losing one's life for a person he loves. Also you showed me how unnerving my muttering can be. And, I do not pay attention to the here and now, but you do. You are a force of gravity for me, Lucy."

"What?" Lucy exclaimed, "Gravity? So, you *do* believe in gravity?"

"Well of course there's gravity, when you need it. Myself, I can take it or leave it. Though, it is useful for tea parties."

"What are you talking about?" Lucy asked.

"Gravity has its limitations like everything else. How do you think we flew through time?" Wilbur chuckled softly.

"Well, didn't we use those jellyfish liquid mirrors?" Lucy asked.

"No, Lucy. We flew on your thoughts. I watched your thoughts stream and trail from your mind and it was like being blinded by ribbons of colored light. You have more magic in you than any being I have ever met."

"Are you serious?" Lucy's mouth was dry and there was a creepy crawly feeling on her neck. "That's scary. So I'm not normal?"

Wilbur touched her hand. "No one is normal in the way the word is used on earth. Everybody has magic in them. Sometimes, it sleeps for one's whole life. Your magic flowered and freed your imagination from all constraints. And that, dear Lucy, is what sent us up in the sky like happy balloons."

"What about the Navigator? Didn't it guide us?"

"Oh yes, my gadgets and I do take a lot of the responsibility for the success of our journey."

"Phew," said Lucy. "I don't want to be all *that* powerful. So, do you think I'll say the right things in my presentation?"

Wilbur put a paw on her shoulder and smiled. "Anything you say will be right, because these are your memories. Your greatest gift is your zeal. It is what makes your thoughts real."

Lucy pressed his paw against her cheek. "Thank you, Wilbur."

"It's time, isn't it, Lucy?"

Lucy nodded and began to cry. "Will I ever see you again?"

Wilbur's voice was barely a whisper. "I have a feeling you will not need my help again."

"But can't I drop in for a visit or text you?" She asked.

Wilbur nodded toward his house. "Go on, now. Run inside and find your necklace."

Lucy found her flash drive on the table beside the Dispatcher. She grabbed it and ran to the doorway.

Wilbur sat in his chair smiling at her.

She held her flash drive high over her head and called, "Look, Wilbur, I found it."

She leapt off the front steps but she never got the chance to say goodbye to him. She was sent hurtling round and round, spinning through blue light, through the petals of a blue rose.

Lucy saw Wilbur's smiling face for the last time and heard him whisper, "I will be in your heart forever."

The light went out, the petals closed and she landed on both feet with a thump on the path she had taken into the woods. She walked across the lawn toward her house. Lucy looked back at the woods and wondered if she would be able to find Wilbur again if she tried. She untied the sweater that had kept him warm and pushed her face into it. His sweet smell and bubbly warmth lived in every crevice and strand of wool. She ached for him.

"Wilbur," said Lucy, looking at the sky, "wherever you are right now, I miss you so much it hurts to breathe. I'll never forget you or stop loving you."

As sad as she was she knew Wilbur had been right. He *would* be in her heart forever. Wherever she was, she would know exactly what he would say to her in any situation.

She could almost hear him now saying, "It will not hurt forever, dear Lucy. Stop dawdling. You have important things to do."

Chapter 18

The Presentation

The morning of the presentations was a real fall day. It was Lucy's favorite kind of day, both warm and cool, when the air smells like crushed acorns. Outside the school, yellow and orange leaves drifted across the pavement.

There was a hushed feeling in Miss Lang's classroom. The yellowed shades turned the light in the room the color of parchment. Lucy knew something magical was about to happen. She turned around in her seat. Sam sat at his desk with his eyes closed and his fingers interlaced.

"Are you meditating or something?" Lucy whispered.

"Shush," he said, without opening his eyes. "She's coming."

"How do you know?"

"I told you yesterday," said Sam. "I just *do*"

The light seemed brighter when Miss Lang floated into the room. She stood smiling in front of the class.

"Today each of you will whisk us away from this room to another place and time. Don't be nervous. Just breathe and let your enthusiasm carry you along."

Miss Lang pulled a child-sized chair to the front of the room opposite the podium and sat down. Her clipboard and pencil lay in her lap. An image of Wilbur making notations on his pad entered Lucy's mind.

"Now," said Miss Lang. "Who wants to be first?"

Lucy's hand shot up.

"Great, come on up, Lucy, and help us see five great paintings through your eyes."

Lucy took a deep breath and walked to the podium. She inserted her flash drive into the school's computer. Although she was a little nervous, she remembered what Vincent had said to her.

"When you are scared, throw yourself headlong into your work. It might feel as though you are stepping off a cliff, but once you get going the momentum will carry you along."

Here goes, Lucy thought.

"My presentation is about how you can see the personalities of artists by studying their paintings. I looked at five paintings for such a long time that now the artists feel like my friends. I hope they will come alive for you too."

She clicked the remote control and Sandro's *Primavera* spread across the screen like a tapestry of bright colors.

"My grandmother gave me a copy of this painting so I have always wondered about it," said Lucy. "Sandro Botticelli painted it in 1480. The colors are so beautiful and bright that they remind me of jewels. There are a hundred different kinds of flowers on the grass. I can just imagine Sandro walking in fields choosing just the right flowers for this painting and drawing them in the hot sun. The goddesses of springtime are dancing. I think this artist must have been a very happy person because this is a painting bursting with joy."

Lucy stopped for a minute to catch her breath. She hoped she was saying the right things and then she remembered sitting in Wilbur's garden asking him what would happen if she said something wrong in her presentation.

"Anything you say will be right because these are your memories."

Lucy clicked the remote button and Jacopo's gigantic *Four Women* hovered on the edge of the screen, giving the impression that at any moment they might topple into the classroom. The students gasped- the size of the women, the mystery of their hushed conversation, and the clashing colors of their dresses-made this painting overwhelming.

"This painting by the artist, Jacopo Pontormo, shocked everyone because it was so different from other paintings at this time. People might have thought he was strange because his style was so surprising. The women are very long and they seem close enough to fall into our room. The colors are very different from Botticelli's red and green. The pink and orange colors clash with each other. I think the painting is wonderful because it is strange and interesting. I bet the artist was brave because he wasn't afraid to try new things. Maybe he was fun to be with."

Next, came Vincent's *Starry Night*. Its whorls of blue and orange blazed on the screen. "Vincent Van Gogh painted *Starry Night* in 1889 when he was in a hospital for people with emotional problems. I think *Starry Night* is full of the feelings of the artist. It

146

shows the sky rolling like huge waves over a little village. If you look very carefully, you will see that everything is painted with choppy, curving lines of thick paint."

Lucy had an idea.

She asked Miss Lang. "Would it be okay if everyone comes up to the screen? You can see really interesting details up close."

Miss Lang nodded and the students crowded around the painting.

Lucy said, "Even though there's no lightning, I think this is a stormy painting because of all the movement of the sky and the twirling moon and stars."

Her classmates were completely awed by the painting. They waited for Lucy to keep going.

"One thing that I noticed is that even though the light around the moon and stars is very bright, the small town is still dark. To paint that dark little town under such a huge stormy sky makes me think that Vincent must have been sad and lonely and probably scared."

Her friends nodded in agreement.

Then Starry Night was replaced by Michelangelo's powerful figure of God.

"This is Michelangelo's *God creating the Sun and Moon* on the Sistine ceiling. The whole ceiling is covered with enormous figures that look like sculptures flying in front of the sky. The ceiling is so energetic that I think Michelangelo might have been quite emotional and very brilliant."

The children went back to their seats.

At last, Lucy came to Leonardo's *Mona Lisa*. She took a minute to think about the important things Leonardo had taught her. She left the podium and stood in front of the screen so that she could both face the class and turn to face the painting.

"This is Leonardo da Vinci's portrait of a woman called *Mona Lisa*. Leonardo's real name was Leonardo da Vinci di Piero and he came from the town of Vinci so it's wrong to call him 'da Vinci,' because all the other people in the town are also 'da Vinci's.'"

"This painting is different from all the other portraits I have seen because she is so mysterious. Everyone talks about her famous smile, but she is really smiling more with her eyes than her mouth. I think Leonardo thought that the eyes show who a person really is. The coolest thing about the painting is that her eyes follow you no matter where you go in the room"

While everyone moved around the room testing this idea, Lucy suddenly felt someone breathing behind her. She glanced over her shoulder and nearly fainted. Lisa sighed and winked at her.

I must be hallucinating. Maybe, I've got jet lag.

"Stop it," said Lucy. "Please go back to being asleep!"

She whipped around to see if anybody else had seen it. Only Sam looked stricken. He was on his feet and as pale as a ghost. Blinking, he pointed at something in the painting. Lucy turned around and then she saw it- a girl and a little dog were walking on the little bridge in the landscape behind Lisa on the right.

Wilbur should have warned me about this, thought Lucy. *I could have had a stroke and Miss Herbert would have to come back and breathe on me again.*

It all happened in less than a second and then the painting froze. Lucy had to fight the urge to laugh. How had Wilbur done it?

Lucy remembered that evening in Leonardo's studio when he had told her, "I can paint anything. I could even paint you and Wilbur walking on one of those paths if I wanted to."

That was the end of Lucy's presentation. Sam was smiling at her. *He knows,* she thought. *I'm glad he knows.* She bowed and everyone clapped and cheered. Miss Lang stood up, smiling her brightest smile.

As Lucy was bending over to pull out her flash drive, Miss Lang whispered in her ear, "Welcome back to the here and now, Lucy."

Sam scrawled a note and slapped it onto Lucy's desk.

"We need to talk."

Sam and Lucy did not say a word to each other on the bus ride home. They wanted to save this most important conversation until they were by themselves with no interruptions. Finally, the bus squealed to a stop in front of their houses and they jumped down from the high step.

Lucy asked, "Do you remember anything strange happening in the last twenty four hours?"

"I heard you calling my name from far away in the middle of the night," he said. "I thought I was dreaming, but I tried to answer you with my thoughts. Did you hear me?"

"Wow that is amazing and so cool," said Lucy. "Yes, I heard you. You helped me a lot. Do you realize what this means?"

Sam shrugged his shoulders. "No, should I?"

"Yes, you're the communications expert. It means that our wavelengths are connected, Sam!"

"Fascinating, see I told you you're a high frequency thinker. That was you with the little dog in the landscape of the *Mona Lisa?* You found a Wise One and he took you back there?"

"Yes," she said, "I was there."

"So you found the door to magic land?"

"There is no door to magic land, only filmy curtains," she said.

"How do you know that?"

Lucy smiled mysteriously and said, "Walk home with me and I'll tell you a story."

The End

COMING SOON

BOOK 2 IN THE LUCY NIGHTINGALE ADVENTURE SERIES

On a trip to Paris with her parents, Lucy meets Anna, a girl who has a very good reason to steal the Mona Lisa. Her husband in her first life paid for it, but Leonardo never gave it to him. Instead, he took it to France and there it has remained, until now. In a harrowing adventure, in which Lucy and Anna are chased through the underground tunnels of Paris, shot at by the French police, and locked in the crypt of a Notre Dame, Lucy helps return the painting to it's rightful owner.

COMING SOON

**BOOK 2 IN THE LUCY NIGHTINGALE
ADVENTURE SERIES**

On a trip to Paris with her parents, Lucy meets Anna, a girl who has a very good reason to steal the Mona Lisa. Her husband in her first life paid for it, but Leonardo never gave it to him. Instead, he took it to France and there it has remained, until now. In a harrowing adventure, in which Lucy and Anna are chased through the underground tunnels of Paris, shot at by the French police, and locked in the crypt of a Notre Dame, Lucy helps return the painting to it's rightful owner.

LUCY NIGHTINGALE, MASTER ART THIEF

OR,

HOW I RETURNED THE MONA LISA TO ITS RIGHTFUL OWNER

Chapter I

Traveling Toward the Adventure

My name is Lucy Nightingale, detective, explorer, and dare devil. I am a successful sixth grader and a magnet for hair-raising adventures. I have faced flesh-eating monsters, fixed magic gadgets, traveled through three dimensions, and performed stunts that would send James Bond running for the hills. I've learned that you can have one adventure after another if you know how to look. So, I advise you to pay attention to everything I'm going to say, or else one day the unknown might creep up behind you and bite your head off. In my case, I'm always on the lookout for the odd anomaly and adventures seem to be snow balling toward me so I have decided to make a permanent record of my life. The following is a true account of my most recent adventure.

. . . .

CPSIA information can be obtained at www.ICGtesting.com
Printed in the USA
LVOW02s0518040814

397276LV00001B/1/P

9 780996 088527